AMISH TRUTH BE TOLD

PEACE VALLEY AMISH SERIES

BOOK 1

RACHEL STOLTZFUS

TABLE OF CONTENTS

ACKNOWLEDGMENTS

I have to thank God first and foremost for the gift of my life and the life of my family. I also have to thank my family for putting up with my crazy hours and how stressed out I can get as I approach a deadline. In addition, I must thank the ladies at Global Grafx Press for working with me to help make my books the best they can be. And last, I thank you, for taking the time to read this book. God Bless!

CHAPTER ONE

Caleb Miller's neck veins bulged out as he yelled at his wife, Annie. "*Nee*, wife! You need to quit working at that shop! Sell it!" Completely in the grips of his frustration and anger, Caleb set his coffee mug down hard on the table's scarred wood surface. As the cup made impact with the hard wood, the force behind the slam caused the sturdy clayware to shatter.

As the cup broke into several pieces, the hot, black coffee within splashed over Caleb's hand, wrist and the table's clean surface. "Awww, look at what you made me do! Naomi, get the cloth and clean this up, right now!" Standing, Caleb raised his fist over his head as he glared at Annie.

Annie, seeing the large, raised fist, took a step back, then stopped. *Nee.* I can't show him fear. Standing her ground, she allowed her eyes to take in details of Caleb's appearance. His eyes were bulging, distorted by his anger. His shoulders pulled up toward his ears—he would soon be complaining of a sore neck.

"Caleb, please listen." In contrast to her husband's yelling, Annie's voice was quiet, although it held a quaver that betrayed strong emotion. "We planned to have a *gut* harvest of the wheat and corn, but *Gott* had other plans. He sent too much rain, then not enough. I won't go into our finances because you know them probably better than I do. What I want to point out is that, as your wife, I want to stand next to you, bringing in some money. I'm the shop owner, and I have two other workers. We get lots of business, which means my shop is popular. I cannot quit and close it. I'd put two other women out of work and, in this economic. . ."

Caleb growled, signaling his impatience with Annie's explanation. "Annie, you are my wife! Women should stay at home and raise the children. . . because *Gott* made them inferior. All you can do is take care of this house and keep watch over Naomi. I expect you to tell me when you have a plan for closing that blasted store! Daughter, are you finished cleaning that table? You are no better than your *mamm*."

Naomi, long used to her *daed*'s clueless insults, still felt this one to her core. Closing her eyes, she gripped the wet cloth and hurried back to the sink, rinsing it out. Clenching her full lips tightly together, she bit back words of anger. "*Mamm*, may I begin clearing up from supper? I need to finish my current quilting order because it's due to my customer in less than two weeks."

"*Ja*. We'll work together. Caleb, we'll speak about this later on." Annie refused to allow her husband to ride over her plans and dreams. She had worked hard to get her quilt shop started and nobody was going to take it away from her, unless it was *Gott*'s will. Waiting until Caleb had gone back to the barn to finish the last of his day's work, she made sure the door was closed before she began speaking quickly. "Naomi, we aren't closing the Quilt Place. Don't you worry about that. We've worked too hard to give up now."

"*Ja*, but *mamm*, why does he talk this way? He puts you and me down and it hurts!" Naomi swiped her soapy hand over her cheek, brushing hot tears away.

Annie was quiet for several seconds, thinking. "He grew up in a time when our *Ordnung* was much more conservative. It's what he's used to. His *daed* was even more strict, if you can imagine that."

"Did *grossdaudi* allow grandmother to work? Or was she restricted to taking care of the house and children because '*Gott* made her inferior?'" The tone of Naomi's voice was heavily sarcastic as she spoke. She glanced through the kitchen window, keeping an eye out for her *daed*.

"Naomi, please be careful. These are your grandparents we're talking about. . . though I agree with you about their beliefs. We are not inferior. We are just as able as any man is." Drawing in a deep, calming breath, Annie glanced quickly outside the window, then continued. "We are supposed to be valued in our homes, daughter. Your *daed*, his brothers and the rest of his family have taken the leadership role too seriously. If you look at other families here in Peace Valley, you'll notice that the husbands and wives are actual partners with each other. The wives have their own businesses, such as baking and selling their goodies at the market or quilting as you do. A few even work outside the. . . oh, he's coming in." As the back door opened, Annie shifted into another topic. ". . . So, because we will be hosting the Sunday service in two weeks, you, your sisters and I will need to begin cleaning the house top to bottom."

Naomi was so grateful that her *mamm* could shift topics so quickly. Drying the dishes and putting them away, she nodded. "*Ja*. Okay. When will we start?"

"Monday. *Ja*, Monday. That will give us time to get every room in the house and make it ready for services."

"It's time for devotionals." Caleb's low voice rumbled from the living room as he held up his worn Bible.

"We're coming, husband." Annie finished wiping surfaces down, then looked around. The kitchen gleamed. "Okay, let's go."

"I want to talk about Ephesians, Chapter five." Caleb began reading the familiar chapter. When he had finished, he looked closely at Annie, who was praying. "Wife, husbands are supposed to love their wives and wives are expected to be submissive to their husbands. Their *kinner* are expected to obey their parents and honor them."

"*Ja*. I understand. We are submissive to our husbands here. Our children obey us and do as we command them. If they sin, we punish them. Caleb, if you'll look at our children, you'll see that they have obeyed you and me. We have rarely had problems with them."

The devotional session ended when Naomi pointed out that she and Annie both held Caleb in high esteem. "*Daed*, I see you as being strong and wise. I see *mamm* as being a complement to you, helping you whether things are good or bad for us. And that makes me want to honor you. As I grew up, I saw my brothers and sisters all had the same opinion of you. We all wanted to grow up and follow your examples."

Caleb was grateful for the calm and, while he wanted to use the moment to press Annie again, something held him back. Smiling at Naomi, he pointed to her quilting room. "Go. That quilt won't sew itself."

Smiling, Naomi stood and, giving her parents quick kisses, she skipped to her quilting studio. As she hurried in, she released a quiet sigh of relief. Tonight's devotional could have gone completely off the rails. Closing her eyes, she thanked *Gott* that everyone had stayed calm as they discussed His Word.

As she worked, piecing quilt pieces together and sewing them with her sewing machine, she thought. *Helpmeet*. Partner. Loved by husbands as Christ loved His church. So, *mamm*, her friends and I can still work outside the home and still not violate *Gott*'s law or our *Ordnung*.

How do I learn more? Who do I talk to? Quickly cutting the sewing thread to release the row of quilt pieces from the machine, she vowed to think more about their situation. Because seeing *daed* raise his fist at *mamm* really didn't feel like love. Conscious of the sounds in the rest of the house, Naomi continued to work. Soon, the sounds of her parents quieted down. They had gone upstairs to bed. Yawning,

Naomi finished sewing the second row of quilt pieces together, then began to straighten out her studio, putting things where they belonged. Blowing out the lantern, she moved quietly through the rest of the house and made sure everything was securely locked up.

After brushing her teeth and showering, she combed out her long hair, still thinking.

Maybe I can talk to Bishop or to Deacon King. The deacon would be easier to approach and talk to. In her room, Naomi stood in front of her window, peering out at the dark, star-studded sky, praying about her family's situation. She knew she wanted to have the freedom to make the choices she would need to make with her future husband, rather than be constrained by what she believed was an outdated belief. Lying down, she thought of her boyfriend, Jethro Yoder. She had dated a couple of Amish boys before beginning to see Jethro. Thinking back, she remembered, even then, knowing she wanted a partner who would view and treat her as an equal in their marriage. Sitting back up, she leaned her back against her pillow. Her smooth forehead creased as she tried to remember the word that the English used in connection to not allowing women to be equals. Giving up, she opened her stand-up closet, where she had stored her old textbooks.

Looking for her notebook, she leafed back to one of the last assignments she had turned in. "*Ja*, here it is. Miss Mary had us work on an assignment about the differences between the Amish and the English." Opening the notebook, she began reading the essay. "Men and women, *ja*, here it is . . . Men and women are viewed as more equal in English communities, although women still lag . . . There it is! 'Sexism' is the word I want!" Dropping the notebook on her bed, Naomi grabbed her dictionary and looked up the definition for 'sexism.'

"The belief that one gender, almost always the male, is superior to the female, which enables him to dominate in almost every area of life. Sexist discrimination in the US in past years has kept many women from achieving the opportunities they want."

As she read quietly, her words slowed down. Sitting back on her bed with her dictionary in her hands, she thought. So it is in Amish life as well. Our men, *daeds* and husbands are acting on the assumption that they are superior to us. And that's why *daed* is acting as he is toward *mamm*. Because he believes she is inferior to him. Once we go to work tomorrow, I want to show this to *mamm*. She needs to know where *daed*'s beliefs come from. With that decision made, she slipped her dictionary and notebook into her carryall so she could show them to her *mamm* the next morning.

Yawning again, she slid under the covers, ready for sleep. Unfortunately, her sleep that night was troubled, punctuated by near-nightmares featuring her parents fighting, with her *daed* striking her *mamm*. After one particularly vivid dream, Naomi sat up, gasping wildly as she tried to come out of the nightmare. Looking around, she touched the cool wall of her bedroom, trying to orient herself back to reality. "It was a bad dream, that's all."

Hearing a sound from downstairs, she looked at her alarm. Seeing that it was almost time to get up, she fell back onto her pillow and groaned softly. "I need more sleep!" She sat up, feeling reluctant to leave her bed when she remembered her decision of the night before. Slipping out of bed, she made her bed and got dressed.

Combing her hair and arranging it in a braided bun, she settled her *kapp* on her head. In the kitchen, she set her carryall against the wall, out of the way of both of her parents. "*Gut* morning, *mamm*. How are you?"

"I'm *gut*, how are. . ." Annie paused, seeing the circles under Naomi's sleepy eyes. ""Ach, you didn't sleep well, did you?"

"*Nee*. Where is *daed*? In the barn?"

"*Ja*. What's wrong?"

While Annie's and Naomi's voices were quiet, they communicated the tension of the situation. "After I went to bed last night, I was thinking." Naomi's words were soft and rushed because she wanted to get them out as fast as possible. "I looked for one of my last essays. It was on sexism. We don't have time right now because *daed* will be back inside soon. But what he's doing is the exact definition of sex discrimination. I have the books in my carryall,* and I'll show you on the way to the store."

Annie was stunned. She realized the level of thought Naomi had put into their situation. "You really want to do something about this, *ja*?" As Naomi nodded, she went on, feeling the pressure of time. "Ours isn't the only family experiencing this. I'll tell you more on the way to the shop. Meanwhile, I see that *daed* is coming back. Get the bacon going, please."

She and Naomi were uncharacteristically quiet as they got breakfast ready. Annie stirred the scrambled eggs and oatmeal as Annie worked on the bacon. Looking up, she smiled quietly at Caleb as he stomped his feet on the outside door mat.

After breakfast, Caleb complimented Annie and Naomi. "*Gut* breakfast. I will be back for supper. We'll be working at the Stoltzfus farm on their harvest, so I'll have dinner over there. It's the last harvest of the season, so we'll be done within a week or two." Giving Annie a rough caress on her arm, he left.

Annie shook her head. She loved the man, even though his

beliefs seemed to be stuck back in the 50s. She laughed quietly as she thought, the 1850s.

"What's funny, *mamm*?" Naomi's dark eyes were large with curiosity.

"I love your *daed* with all my heart, daughter. But he has some real old-fashioned beliefs. I laughed because he is stuck in the 50s."

"The 1950s? But *mamm*, that's like, almost 60 years ago. Even then, *daeds* were more, uh, evolved?"

"Annie began laughing. "*Nee*, Naomi. The 1850s! It's funny in a sad way. I laugh because, if I didn't have that, I would be crying. And I am so amazed at your insight. You caught onto our situation so quickly last night, because you are living it. . . let's get the dishes done and kitchen cleaned up so we can go. We'll talk on the way to the shop."

After Naomi and Annie cleaned the kitchen and packed their lunches, they left for the shop. While Annie guided the team of horses, Naomi read the definition she had found in her dictionary. Then, she explained how she had chosen her previous boyfriends and current one. "*Mamm*, I know that I don't want to go through what *daed* does to you. I love him, but *ja*, he is stuck back in a very old-fashioned way of thinking. My first boyfriend could have been *daed*'s son, for his way of thinking. That's why I only dated him for a few months. My second boyfriend. . . well, he talked *gut* about believing that women should be able to make decisions. But when it came down to talking about what his future wife would be 'allowed' to do, I found out that she wouldn't be able to do much more than bake or quilt and sell what she made. When we talked about it, I brought up your shop and he told me, 'I would make my future wife sell the shop or quit working outside the home. Once we get married, she gives up her rights to work away from home.' *Mamm*, that's the night that I broke up with him. When he brought me home, I told him I wouldn't be seeing him anymore. He tried to get into an argument with me. I jumped out of the buggy and ran, even though I twisted my ankle. He wasn't going to do anything to me!"

Annie was stunned. Naomi had never shared this with her. "Wha. . . Naomi! Why didn't you say anything?"

Naomi was silent. "I don't know. I was embarrassed and ashamed."

"Daughter, please, don't ever be ashamed when someone does something to you! You are a strong young woman, just like your sisters. You did the right thing by running away from him. But please, if ever anyone does anything like that to you again, tell me!"

Naomi nodded, feeling shock. "*Mamm*, I just wasn't sure if you or *daed* would believe me. And, I thought that, by bringing up you and your shop, that I brought all of his words and actions on myself."

"*Nee*, Naomi! His beliefs. . . and his insecurities. . . made him act out against you. It wasn't your fault. It's too late for us to go to the elders now. Please promise me that, if Jethro acts like this, you'll tell your *daed* and me right away."

"*Ja*, I will. Jethro hasn't ever tried to get physical with me. I don't think he will, either, because, when we've talked, he has agreed with my position on how wives can be the equals of their husbands. *Mamm* . . . before Jethro and I started dating, I took the time to find out what he believed. I didn't bother with that with John. And I regret that. Well, I nearly regret it. I learned what I don't want in a relationship with my future husband."

"I shouldn't ask, but is there a possibility that you and Jethro might marry?"

Naomi blushed because parents normally wouldn't find out about their children's plans to marry until the couple got engaged. "We. . . we've talked about it, but we haven't really made a decision yet. Besides, we still need to get to know each other much better."

Annie was quiet for several minutes. Rousing, she realized they were almost at her shop. "We're almost at work. Thankfully, Leora won't be here for about half an hour. That should give us time to make sure we can talk about what you brought to work with you. Because I really want to know."

***

Inside the shop, after preparing the cash register and putting sales flyers on the counter, Annie and Naomi sat, discussing what Naomi had dug out of her closet. "*Mamm*, sexism is the belief that one gender, usually the men, think they are superior to us. This leads to sex discrimination. . ."

"What is sex discrimination?" Annie's brow crinkled in confusion.

"That's when people—usually men—stop women who are just as qualified as they are from sharing in the same opportunities. Like getting a job or even having the right to work at all."

Annie's first reaction was a widening of her eyes as she understood what Naomi was saying. Then, her being radiated sadness as her eyes dimmed. "You mean. . . like what your *daed* is trying to do to me."

RACHEL STOLTZFUS

CHAPTER TWO

Naomi's mouth filled with a sour taste as she nodded. "*Mamm*, I really hate seeing you like this. It's hard, I know. But we can keep on doing what we're doing. Remember, your store gives so much good to so many here! Leora works here. The women can sell their quilts on consignment, which helps them earn money for their families. And the English tourists love the quilts! *Ja*, you're unusual because you own your business. But other Amish women own their businesses, too."

Annie smiled, grateful for Naomi's sensitive words. Feeling her love for her daughter welling over, she gave her a rare hug. "*Ja*, that is true, isn't it? You know, before I opened my shop, I worked out of the house. As more and more women brought quilts for me to sell, Caleb got upset because they took up so much space. He told me, "Just find a building on the edge of town and rent that. Sell from there." Another memory bubbled up to the surface of Annie's mind. "Then, he said. . . he said,

"I don't mind you doing this because it's women's work."

Naomi's eyebrows came together as she frowned. With great difficulty, she refrained from saying anything, knowing it would be disrespectful of her *daed*. "Am I right in remembering that, another time, he told you, "Your business has kept us from going under when things haven't gone well with the crops?"

"*Ja*! He did! More than once! Daughter, we'd better get ready for our work day. It will be busy because I have that promotion starting today. And look, there's Leora."

The bells on the front door tinkled as Leora came in. "*Gut* morning! It will be a warm day today. We should have lots of tourists coming in."

***

While Annie and Naomi were discussing Caleb's issues with Annie's shop, another Peace Valley family was having its difficulties. Lizzie Lapp had served as the manager of the Peace Valley Quilt Place until her husband, Wayne, had forced her to resign her position. This morning, Lizzie had suggested that she return to work on a part-time basis, so they could help their daughter and granddaughter with medical expenses. "Barbara's *boppli* has that asthma now, and the supplies are expensive. Her husband's income doesn't quite stretch to cover the nebulizer, which the baby needs so she can breathe better on bad days."

"They're borrowing one from the clinic, aren't they?" At Lizzie's nod, he shook his head. "*Nee.* You stay home. Period. This is where you belong, taking care of home, meals, Leora and our grandbabies."

"But. . ."

"No buts! You remember that last time we discussed this!" As he yelled, Wayne raised his fist in a threatening way.

Lizzie remembered only too well the beating she had gotten from Wayne. It had been the first time he'd ever hit her, although his temper and raised voice had long been an issue between the two of them. Backing up and moving into the spacious living room, she raised her hands in a defensive way, shaking her head. "*Nee!* Don't hit me, Wayne! I'll go to the elders if you do!"

Leora came into the kitchen at that point. Seeing her *daed*'s raised fist, she dropped her black cape. "*Daed! Nee!* Don't hit her!" She backed up and, standing next to Lizzie, she wrapped both arms around her mother's shoulders.

Wayne, seeing his wife and daughter standing huddled together, dropped his arm and his attitude. "Wife, you just remember that I make the decisions here! I've decided you're not working outside the house, no matter what! If you want to earn more money, give quilts to Annie for her to sell. Bake. But you're not working outside the home! And Leora, the day you marry, you're staying at home, in your husband's home. No need for you to work outside the home, either." He was about to raise the point that she could work from home, but seeing the defiant, angry look on Leora's face, he decided to wait. "Don't think that Annie Miller's going to have that shop for much longer. I've been talking with Caleb. He'll get her to close it. Leora, that means you'll have no choice but to work from home." Slamming his straw hat on his head, he gave a stern nod and left through the kitchen door, slamming it behind him.

"*Mamm*, did he hit you?" Leora allowed her eyes to roam over Lizzie's face and neck.

"*Nee*. You came in at the right time. I wish he didn't have this notion that women aren't supposed to work outside the home! Your sister needs that machine for baby Anna."

"He won't even let you work part-time?"

Lizzie shook her head. "Well, there's nothing for it but to finish that quilt and take it to Annie's store. Would you please let her know that I'll be donating quilts on consignment?"

"*Ja, mamm*, you know I will." Leora felt her head cover and hair, making sure they were smooth and straight on her head. "I'd better go now. I'll be home before supper. But tomorrow, Annie has an all-day sale, so I may not be home until shortly after you put supper on the table. I have to be at work by nine tomorrow morning."

"*Gut*. You go. Just remember, bring your pay home and I'll put it away for you. Let me know if you need anything from your pay so you can buy it."

"I will. Bye, *mamm*." Leora waved as she left the house. On her walk to the store, she thought, wondering why some men were so stern about women working. I'll talk to Naomi on our breaks and see what she says. She knew she could never bring up the fact that her *daed* threatened physical violence against her *mamm*. To do so would bring shame on her family. Hurrying up the porch steps to the shop, she forced herself to smile and think of a happy topic.

Annie's words about the English tourists was prophetic. She, Naomi, Leora and their other two employees were kept busy, running from the back room to the cash register, ringing up sales and wrapping up quilts and smaller blankets.

"Naomi, you and Leora take the first break today. Rebecca and Miriam, you'll get the second break today." Annie rushed by, a quilt and blanket set in her arms ready to wrap and ring up.

"Let's go to the back. I brought some cookies and milk we can enjoy." Naomi grinned at her friend, feeling better about the day.

"Naomi, why do some of the men here don't like letting us women work outside the home? *Mamm* wants to come back to the shop, but *daed* won't let her. He says she can earn money from home if she wants to. Oh, she's going to send a quilt with me in a couple weeks."

Naomi finished chewing her cookie before answering. Wiping her mouth, she thought. "Well, *mamm* and I talked about sexism and sex discrimination. Remember that paper that Miss Mary had us write in our last year of school? Mine was about how women have to deal with sexism."

"*Ja*, now I remember! I think men and women are equal. We can do a good job earning money for our families."

"*Ja*, we can! *Daed* still wants *mamm* to close the store. She doesn't want to, because we employ you, Rebecca and Miriam. Women in Peace Valley can make quilts at home, then sell them here. So everyone wins."

"Well. . . everyone except for the men. They think." Leora's voice was droll as she threw that into the conversation.

Naomi, about to take a drink of milk, put her glass back on the table and began laughing hard. "*Ja*, that's for sure and for certain, isn't it? I don't want to disrespect *daed* or your *daed*. But. . ." Her voice dropped to a whisper. "It's so ridiculous. It's like they're afraid that we'll show them up or something."

Leora's grin faded. "Naomi, listen. *Daed* was saying that he's been working with your *daed* to make your *mamm* close the store. Your *mamm* needs to know that."

Naomi's giggles stopped, just as if someone had shut off a spigot. "What?" Her eyes roamed around the small, neat and comfortable break room. In her mind, she pictured the bright, spacious display and sale area. This was her second home!

She'd grown up spending her days with her *mamm*, beginning to work for her after she finished school at fourteen. Looking at the remaining cookies in the bag, she zipped the bag shut, no longer feeling hungry. Covering her travel mug, she stored the rest of her milk back in the small refrigerator. "Leora, are you sure? Did you misunderstand your *daed*?"

"*Nee*. He said so this morning, that he's been talking with your *daed*. He said that your *mamm* won't have the store for much longer. We need to let your *mamm* know!"

"Can you stay a little late tonight so you can talk to my *mamm*?"

Leora grimaced. "I wish I could! I promised *mamm* I'd be home in time to fix supper with her. *Daed*'s mood wasn't very good because I heard her ask him about coming back here part-time. She wants to help Barbara out with the *boppli*'s medical expenses. He said no, that she could bring quilts here to sell."

"We want her quilts. But does he realize what harm he'll do if he and my *daed* succeed in getting *mamm* to close her store? Okay. Denki. I'll tell *mamm* tonight so she's warned and can be ready."

After storing their snacks back in the refrigerator, both girls went back to the sales floor to relieve the two other employees. As they worked, straightening out displays and cleaning counters, they were both quiet.

Annie noticed the new moods Leora and Naomi appeared to

be in. Pulling them in close to her during a small lull, she referred to their change. "I hope you'll be able to greet guests to the store and make them feel welcome. What happened while you were on break?"

Naomi looked at Leora, who shrugged. "*Mamm*, I see new customers walking up. I'll let you know tonight, okay?"

Annie had no choice but to accept that—several customers came into the shop, each veering to different areas of the store and asking several questions. The remainder of their day was busy with few lulls. At lunch time, Annie gratefully locked the front door and flipped the door sign to "closed."

Sitting in the back with her daughter and employees, she ate and rested her aching feet. Looking at Naomi and Leora, she was relieved to see they had regained their high spirits. All four girls talked and giggled as they ate, discussing the sing they would be attending on Sunday night.

"*Ja*, Vernon and I will be at the sing. Naomi, will you be there with Jethro?"

"*Ja*, of course! Rebecca, Miriam, what about you?" Naomi's cheeks were flushed as she asked the question.

Miriam nodded, blushing. "*Ja*. John asked me to go at the last sing and I told him I would."

Rebecca was the sole girl with no plans to attend with one of the boys in their community. "*Nee*. I broke up with Abe."

Naomi gasped. "Rebecca, why? You seemed to be getting along so well!"

Rebecca shook her head. "*Nee.*" As she spoke, she absently rubbed her left forearm. "He. . . doesn't like that I work here. He'd rather that I earn money by working from home, like most of our mothers do. He brought it up the last time we got together. He came over to visit on Tuesday or Wednesday night. We got into an argument when I told him that my parents use some of my earnings to pay off the loan at the bank. That I'm happy to be able to help out. Well, he told me I could work from home and I told him I wouldn't earn as much as I do now. He grabbed my arm and tried to twist it and force me to agree to quit working here. . ."

Annie leaned forward and, holding Rebecca's hand, she gently raised the long sleeve of her dress. Seeing the livid, purple bruise on her employee's arm, she gasped. "Rebecca! Did you tell your parents about this?"

"*Ja*, after I broke up with Abe and told him never to come back." She chuckled slightly, then her voice caught. "He wasn't. . . wasn't too happy when he left."

"Rebecca, does that hurt? Would you like some ice or something for it?" Naomi stood up. "We still have some time for lunch before we need to open back up."

"*Nee*, I'm fine. Denki. *Mamm* has been putting ice and a rub for sore muscles at night, then wrapping it. Today's the first day I've gone without the wrap."

"*Mamm*, I want to tell her about my own experience. Please?"

Annie nodded. "I think we can dispense with our usual custom of courting secrecy for this."

"Rebecca, I had two boyfriends before I began dating Jethro. My first boyfriend was just. . . well, outright firm that he didn't want his future wife working outside the home. We had only been dating for a couple months, so he wasn't too upset when I broke up with him. My second boyfriend talked a good game about supporting our right to help support our families. But, when we talked about marriage, he said he'd 'make' his future wife stop working outside the home. I told him we wouldn't be seeing each other anymore when he pulled into our yard. He tried to get into an argument with me and he tried to grab me. I just jumped out of his buggy and ran into the house. Now, before I begin dating anyone, I find out, for sure and for certain, what a young man believes about his girlfriend or wife working outside the home."

Leora leaned forward. "I do the same."

"Rebecca, Miriam, *mamm* and I talked about sex discrimination and sexism on our way here this morning."

Annie stood, needing to walk while Naomi and the girls talked. She kept her attention on their conversation, ready to jump in if needed. Looking outside the window of the back room, she saw Caleb and Wayne Lapp walking to their buggies. They were deep in conversation. For some reason,

Annie didn't have a good feeling about what she was seeing—she remembered how hard Lizzie Lapp, her previous manager, had tried to continue working outside the home, until the day she had had to stay home, 'sick.' Annie had run into her at the next Sunday's church meeting. Lizzie had a large bruise on her cheek, which she had tried to cover with her black bonnet.

RACHEL STOLTZFUS

CHAPTER THREE

"Lizzie, what happened? Your cheek!" Naomi had been stunned.

Lizzie looked around and, not seeing Wayne, she gestured to the house. "Let's go inside." The meeting had been at the Lapp house that Sunday. "Annie, I am so sorry, but I'm going to have to resign as manager at the shop." Looking down, Lizzie had gulped, seeming to struggle with tears.

"Lizzie, what's wrong? This is about more than just resigning, isn't it?" Annie's intuition had begun to warn her about something bad.

"*Ja*. Close the door, please." After Annie had closed the bedroom door, she joined Lizzie on the side of the bed. "Annie, Wayne hasn't liked it that I work in your shop. He wouldn't like my working in anyone's business. That's. . . well, that's how this happened." With one hand, Lizzie had indicated the livid bruise on her face. "He. . . beat me and now, I have to quit." Turning her face to the side, Lizzie began to cry quietly.

Annie felt sick, knowing her intuition had told her right once again. "Lizzie, I'm so sorry! I hate having to accept your resignation, but we know the *Ordnung* says we're to obey our husbands. Much as I don't like that he used physical force to make you agree. I don't want you to put you in any danger of more beatings. I value your friendship too much." Annie sighed, not wanting to cry. "*Ja.* I accept your resignation. Reluctantly." She had hugged Lizzie, trying to give her what comfort she could. "The shop has been doing very well. I'll be giving you severance pay on top of your regular pay. And you know that, if Wayne felt differently, I would have you back right away."

Lizzie had tried to smile. Carefully wiping tears away, she nodded. "*Ja,* I know. Thank you!"

Looking back around at the girls, Annie slid away from the window. If she could see Caleb, he could see her. Sitting back at the table, she forced her attention to the girls' conversation. I need to tell Annie and Leora what I just saw. When we close tonight. "Girls, we need to finish here and get opened again. It's nearly one and we close at four." By the time the end of the day rolled around, Annie was grateful. Counting the day's receipts and preparing the bank deposit, she reminded the girls to be on time the next day, "It's Saturday tomorrow. That, along with our sale, means we'll be very busy. I will see you here bright and early! Oh, Leora, can you stay for just a minute?"

"I'm sorry, but I promised *mamm* I'd get home as soon as we closed. She and *daed* had a. . . discussion this morning and. . ."

"Okay. But please, listen. I was looking out the back window at lunch today." Annie's words rushed together in her hurry. "I saw Caleb and your *daed*, walking together and having a conversation. They seem to have been buying supplies. Or they met, just to talk."

Leora's eyes widened and her mouth opened as she gasped. "Oh, no! Annie, *daed* said he would be talking to your husband about how to make you close your shop! They must have been talking about that! I'd better go. I'm. . . I'm sorry. I wish I didn't have to tell you that." Turning, she rushed out of the shop and began jogging home.

Annie looked down and grimaced. "No doubt she's right. Naomi, let's go home. We'll get here early and straighten out the rest of the shop and get ready then. We don't need to anger your *daed* any more than he already is. We need to be ready for anything he says or does." Annie was so preoccupied with Leora's news that she nearly forgot to lock the shop.

"*Mamm*! You forgot to lock the door! Here, let me have the key." Naomi made sure the door was secure. "Bank and deposit. If we hurry, we can be in the kitchen before *daed* comes inside."

"Let's go. And, denki." Annie smiled, feeling a little of the tension in her shoulders easing. After depositing the day's earnings, she headed the buggy for home.

***

"Ach, yes! It's only four-thirty! We can start supper—and thank *Gott* I cut the vegetables for the stew already. Come. . . you work on the biscuits and dessert while I cut up the meat and make the stew."

Thirty minutes later, the stew was bubbling and ready to be served. Naomi pulled the biscuits out of the oven just as Caleb came into the kitchen.

"This smells *gut*! Now, this is just what I like to see. My women, working hard at what they are best at. Taking care of the family." With a self-satisfied smile, he ran upstairs to change his shirt and wash his hands.

As he was upstairs, Annie and Naomi exchanged a long gaze that said everything they couldn't say out loud. Annie put her finger over her lips. "Shhh, we'll go outside for a walk after supper and cleaning up."

Naomi, not trusting her words, just nodded. Setting the table, she tensed as she heard her *daed*'s familiar footfalls when he entered the kitchen.

"Stew! One of my favorites! What's for dessert?"

Annie spoke. "Apple pie with ice cream."

During dinner, Naomi didn't contribute much to the conversation. Instead, she simply ate her meal, waiting until she and her *mamm* could go walking.

"Naomi, why aren't you talking? You're normally not this quiet." Caleb took a huge bite of one of her biscuits.

"I'm just thinking about going to pick up quilts from some of the women next week. And about getting together with Leora and Vernon."

"Vernon? Vernon King? He seems to be a good boy. Although his parents seem to have some strange ideas."

"*Daed*? I'm going to start cutting the pie. Are you ready?" Naomi was aware she had brought up a potentially sensitive topic.

"*Ja*, I am. This is *gut*! Who made it?"

"Me." For the first time, Naomi smiled. "Denki." Her pie did taste good.

After cleaning the kitchen, Naomi and Annie went on their walk. Holding flashlights, they walked alongside the road, talking. "*Mamm*, how are you going to deal with *daed*, especially on weekends?" Naomi was seriously worried, especially after learning what she had heard that day.

"I already have tomorrow under control. We'll prepare the meat, fruits and vegetables for supper. Your sister is coming over so your *daed* can have a hot lunch after finishing his work.

He's going over to the Hofstetter's to help them unload benches and tables for the Sunday service, so he's going to be out of the house most of the day. We'll get home again before five and put supper on the table. You are going to open the shop every day next week while I clean the house and do the laundry. In fact, I'm thinking. . . about keeping the shop, but stepping back from day-to-day operation. What would you think of stepping up to become the manager? You're single. You say Jethro is okay with you working outside the house? What would he say about this?"

Naomi was stunned. Looking at her *mamm*, she forgot to breathe for a few seconds. Inhaling audibly, she closed her mouth and blinked as she forced her mind to function. "Umm, oh! Wow! *Ja*, I would be happy to help as manager! But I would need to learn how to take care of all the paperwork. Hiring, pay, firing, all of that."

Annie giggled, feeling nervous. "And Jethro?"

"Jethro would be fine with it. But, just to be sure, I will talk to him the next time we're together. *Mamm*? Will you be in the shop at all or stay home full-time?"

"I would be in the shop at least two days a week, maybe four. I haven't decided whether that would be from noon to close or if I would spend a full day there or not. I'm just trying to make it to where your *daed* stops acting like this."

Something about her mother's last statement bothered Naomi. Looking at the ground, she focused on that as she watched the pool of light from her flashlight. "*Mamm*? I'm going to say something and please, don't get upset. Because I love you."

"I. . . okay. What is it?"

"Why are you trying to placate *daed*? He needs to stop. I'm sorry. I hope that's not disrespectful, but he has been disrespecting you with his threats. I like your idea, because you will get more time away from the shop to relax. But you shouldn't do this just to make him more comfortable."

Annie looked at Naomi and her mouth fell open. Ouch! Out of the mouths of . . . ow! "Well, I have also been thinking about going to talk to the bishop. Or one of the ministers. I want to find out exactly what the *Ordnung* says about our women working out of the home."

It was Naomi's turn to be surprised. Shaking her head, she peered closely at Annie. "About. . . "

"Surely, our district's *Ordnung* allows married women who are working to provide for their families to work, either in or out of the home. I want to find out if your *daed*'s thinking goes against the *Ordnung*. If he needs to adjust his thinking." Annie remembered what she had seen during lunch. "Oh! I forgot about this. During lunch, I was looking outside the window at the back of the store. I spotted your *daed* and Wayne Lapp walking down the street, just talking."

"Okay. . . Oh! He forced Lizzie to quit her job! *Mamm*, this could mean trouble. Do you think they were talking about how to make the shop close?"

Annie's heart squeezed painfully. "I hope not! That's why I want you to think about this manager's position. Don't make a decision right away. If your *daed* is up to something, I want to be ready with a plan. We'd better go back."

The two turned around. "*Mamm,* when do you need a decision?"

"As soon as you get an answer from *Gott* and Jethro. Seriously."

This brought home to Naomi the urgency of her mother's situation. "Okay. I'll be praying about it."

***

The next morning, Naomi worked, moving from counter to stock room and back to the counter. As she did, she mulled over her mother's idea, wondering if she could really manage the shop.

Shortly after lunch, Lizzie Lapp came in, holding a heavy quilt. " Annie, I have several more in the back of my buggy, if I could get some help with them."

Annie sent Leora and Naomi out to help bring the remainder of the quilts in. As they placed them on the shop's counter, several English shoppers crowded around. "Ladies, I still need to price these and write up the description. You'll be able to look at them, possibly on Tuesday. Lizzie, do you want to fill out this consignment paperwork so I can start an account for you?"

Lizzie let out a soft sigh. "Denki! Yes, I will." Moving to the back of the shop, she filled out every page, knowing she had found a compromise that, hopefully, would make Wayne happy. Bringing the sheets of paper to Annie, she looked around while Annie created an account for her on the small computer allowed by the Amish. "Annie, if I can bring in a quilt a month, I would like to do so."

Annie's grin beamed absolute happiness. "*Ja*! Your work is so beautiful and I know it will sell fast. You know my consignment structure—60/40, with you getting the 40 percent. Because these are full-sized quilts, they will be priced at a minimum of $500."

Lizzie's eyes rounded. "You've raised your prices!" In her mind, she was figuring out her 40 percent split and thanking *Gott*. Now, she could give Barbara *gut* news about helping with the nebulizer and medications for her granddaughter.

"*Ja*. My rent has gone up, so I had to raise my quilt prices. If you bring in smaller quilts, such as for dolls or cribs, those are priced lower. Doll quilts are $25 and crib quilts are $125."

Lizzie put her hand over her mouth as tears threatened to overwhelm her.

Annie saw the powerful emotion coming over her old friend.

"Come. Let's go to the back. I'll get you some water." Wrapping her arm around Lizzie's slender waist, she comforted her. Getting a bottle of cold water, she sat her friend down. "What is it?"

"Barbara's youngest has been diagnosed with asthma. The medications are so expensive. I tried to get Wayne to agree to allow me to come back, even part-time and he raised his fist to me. I'm making and selling quilts so I can help Barbara and her husband afford these medications and the nebulizer."

"Oh, my! Of course, I'll help in every way I can. I'm running a big promotion, so you brought your quilts in at just the right time—I'm running low of quilts made here. I'll position them front and center so customers see them. I know they're going to want to buy them!" As Annie chattered, she decided she was going to change the consignment split for Lizzie, from 60/40 to 50/50. Her friendship with Lizzie warranted this, as did Lizzie's family situation. And Lizzie would be the only one who received this split.

As Leora worked outside, she overheard snatches of the conversation between her *mamm* and Annie. As she processed what Lizzie was saying, she solidified a decision in her mind— she was going to go to talk to Jethro and see if she could talk to his *mamm* and *daed*, because something told her that her own *daed*'s treatment of her *mamm* was wrong and against the *Ordnung*.

***

As Leora walked home, she tried to allow the beauty of the spring day to calm her down. Gazing around, she saw the young wheat and corn stalks swaying in the gentle breeze. The sky was endless, seeming to go up forever. And, as she walked, Leora heard and felt the crunch of the rocks under her shoes. Inside the house, she dropped her carryall in her room, washed her hands and ran back downstairs to help Lizzie with supper.

"There you are, daughter! I'm working on the meat, if you'll work on the vegetables and brown the potatoes. Once they are nearly done, add the sliced onions, pepper and salt. I'll let you know when to put the pie into the oven."

Agreeing, Leora worked alongside Lizzie. As they worked, they talked quietly, about their respective days.

"*Ja*, it was busy. You saw when you came in with the quilts. Oh, we've already had one sale! An English tourist bought the Hunter's Star quilt! Several were interested in the Miniature Hearts crib quilt you made, and they'll come back in on Tuesday with money! Annie wants to know how many you can make a month."

Lizzie closed her eyes, sending up a silent prayer of thanksgiving. "Maybe two a month, if I work every day. Oh, thank the Lord!"

After dinner was over, Leora left with Vernon, who had made plans with her to spend the evening together. Before they left, Wayne tried to give Leora a hard time. "Daughter, you're going to see each other tomorrow night at the sing! I want you back in early because we have services tomorrow."

"*Ja*, *daed*, I will be in early. I promise." Leora struggled to keep her frustration out of her voice. Once in the buggy, she sighed.

"That doesn't sound *gut*. What's wrong?"

"Let's wait until we're down the road a bit. *Ja*, this is serious and I'll be asking for your help."

"Oh. Would you like to go and get some milkshakes so we can talk?"

"*Ja*, denki! That would be wunderbaar!" Leora loved pineapple milkshakes—she imagined they tasted how Hawaii looked.

At the milkshake shop, they took their shakes to a table that was set off from the main grouping of tables. "So, what is it?"

Leora swallowed the sweet, icy taste and exhaled nervously. "Vernon, this has to stay strictly between you and me. Please!"

Vernon studied his petite girlfriend. Her green eyes were vivid. "Okay. I promise."

"Denki. Remember that my *mamm* used to manage Annie Miller's quilt shop?" At Vernon's nod, she continued. "*Daed* forced her to quit. He doesn't like his wife to be working outside the home, believes she should be content staying at home. Only. . . my older sister's youngest has been diagnosed with asthma and the medications are expensive. The nebulizer is also expensive. She took several of her quilts into the shop today and it looks like they are going to sell fast."

"Well, it looks like she's found a solution for that, right? What's going on?"

Vernon didn't know it, but he was about to get a life lesson from Leora.

Leora sent a look of disbelief toward ~~Jethro~~ Vernon. Turning around, she looked around the milkshake shop, taking in the other customers, the activity level and the scents of the different milkshakes being prepared. "Vernon . . . really?" Scooting her chair closer to him, she leaned inward. "Come here." Her voice had dropped to a low whisper.

Vernon obeyed, scooting much closer. "What is it?"

"It's not just a matter of *daed* making *mamm* resign from her job at the quilt shop. He did more. He beat her, Vernon. He left her with bruises on her face. And, because she didn't want that treatment again, she gave in. She knows he's going to start working on me. But because our *Ordnung* says that, because I'm unmarried, I can work outside the home as long as my work doesn't violate any part of the *Ordnung*. Vernon, tell me if I'm wrong. Can *daed* force *mamm* to quit her work? Or did he violate the Ordung?"

Vernon's mouth slowly fell open as he fell back against his chair. He shook his head and exhaled with a loud whoosh. "Leora, I am so sorry! I know only what my *daed* has said. Our

Ordnung doesn't say anything specific about married—or single—women working outside the home. I need to ask him about the written part that governs all our districts. But I've never heard tell of anything that said women can't work outside the home. He is definitely violating our *Ordnung* by assaulting your *mamm*."

CHAPTER FOUR

Leora's appetite for her frozen confection disappeared. "Mei *Gott*!" Remembering what Annie had said about seeing her *daed* with Annie's husband came back. "Oh, no. . . Vernon, I think my *daed* is giving Annie Miller's husband ideas about how to force Annie to close the Peace Valley Quilt Place. That might include beating her or even Naomi."

"You think so?"

"For sure and for certain, if he—Mr. Miller— is successful in forcing his wife to close the shop, it could put a lot of us out of business. Even my *mamm*. She is making quilts at home and taking them to the Quilt Place. See, the Quilt Place accepts quilts on consignment and sells them for those women who bring them in. Not having that as an option would hurt those women."

Vernon pressed the heels of his hands into his eyes in reaction. Looking up, he looked outside the large window of the shop, seeing people walking and driving by. "Leora, aren't you afraid of living under your *daed*'s roof?"

Leora thought for a few minutes. As she did, her attention was pulled away by a small English toddler who was determined to run off her energy in the shop. She smiled slightly at the little girl, who was wearing light-purple leggings, a fluffy white-and-purple top and sneakers with flashing red lights in the soles. Feeling Vernon's warm hand on her wrist, she came back to the present. "Oh, uh, *Nee*, not really. When I come into the kitchen or wherever they are and he's been. . . bullying her, he stops when he sees me. I tell him to stop and he does. Stop, that is. I think he's ashamed of what he does, even thought it got him what he wanted."

"Okay, so you're safe. . . for now. About finding out if what he does violates the *Ordnung*, I need to check with *daed*. Do you mind if I do?"

"*Nee*, go ahead."

"He may want to have the elders come and talk to your *daed* if he asks me how I know this."

Leora caught the warning right away. "That doesn't matter. He fears the elders. He is so worried about breaking the *Ordnung* that he orders us not to do anything that will reflect on him! If he knows that someone talked to one of the elders, he may stop."

Vernon ruffled his hair as he thought. Running his hand

back and forth over the top of his head, he was in danger of creating a rat's nest until his hand stopped moving over his head. ""*Ja*, it could make him stop. But I'm thinking my *daed* should not be one of those visiting him. Or he'll think you told one of us."

Leora shivered as she thought of the consequences. "Uh, *ja*. Good point! Denki for listening to me." Pulling the shake back toward her, she began to drink it down before it melted completely.

***

Over the next few days, Leora waited for word from Vernon. She also worried, wondering who would come to visit her *daed*. One morning, as she was on her way to the Quilt Place for work, she realized she was beginning to obsess over the question. Releasing a deep sigh, she sent up a quick prayer then forced herself to take in the beauty around her.

It was full summer and the morning was already warm. Smiling slightly at the caress of the breeze on her cheek, Leora felt herself beginning to relax. A small dimple in her right cheek peeked out as she smiled. Her wavy bangs responded to the slight breeze, moving around her forehead and, as the wind picked up momentarily, flying back over her head covering before setting on her forehead once again.

"Leora! Wait up!"

Leora turned, hearing the pounding of shoes on pavement.

"Vernon! *Gut* morning!"

"*Gut.* . . morning! You walk fast, don't you? I've been calling your name for a minute."

"Oh! I'm sorry! I was trying not to be so obsessed about. . . well, you know. I was rejoicing over the wonders we have all around us."

By now, Vernon had caught his breath. "I just wanted to let you know. I told my *daed* what you told me. He agreed with me. The elders need to visit your *daed*. And that will happen this afternoon or this evening. The deacon and the other minister will visit him. They won't reveal that you're the one who spoke up."

Leora closed her eyes in relief. "I'll be home by then. Will they want to talk to him by himself?"

"*Ja*, I would imagine. They'll probably talk to your *mamm* as well."

Leora stopped. Her vivid green eyes opened wide in fear. "Oh, no! I didn't want her to be involved!"

"She is. She's a victim. When you think about it, you are, too. They have to talk to her and, depending on what she says, they may want to talk to you as well. Leora, don't worry so much! If he knows that he's in danger of being put in the *Meidung*, he may stop forcing his will on your *mamm* and you."

Leora nodded, her mind obviously elsewhere. "Should I say anything to Mrs. Miller?"

Vernon began to ruffle his hair once again, thinking. "You said he might be giving ideas or guidance to Mr. Miller, *ja*? I would tell her something, but in private."

Leora's bright smile made her look even prettier than she already did. "Denki! I will—I don't want to see the shop closed because. . . my *daed* and Mr. Miller aren't willing to come into the 21st century."

"Okay. I'll see you later this week?"

"*Ja*! I'll be there!" Leora kept walking to the shop while ~~Jethro~~ Vernon returned to the market, where he was buying replacement parts for one of the saws.

Leora was almost at the shop when she saw her *daed* driving his buggy in the opposite direction. Forcing herself to smile at him, she waved, trying to seem like a carefree young woman focused on her job.

Wayne saw Leora and, raising his hand from the reins, he waved back. Instead of smiling, he sent a scowl toward his daughter.

Leora, seeing the frown, stopped smiling. Opening the door quickly, she slipped in and tried to forget the image of her *daed*'s face. Seeing that she still had some time, and that the other workers were still not there, she gestured toward Naomi and Annie. "I have some news! Fast! Before the others get here."

In the back of the shop, Annie looked at Leora, wondering what had happened. "What is it?"

"I told Vernon what's been happening with my *daed* and with your husband, Annie. He spoke to his *daed*, who spoke to the bishop and the other elders. My *daed* has violated the *Ordnung* by beating my *mamm*. The deacon and the other minister are going to come to our house later today and talk to my *daed*. Annie, they are aware that my *daed* has been giving your husband suggestions to make you close the shop and stay at home."

Annie was stunned. Looking toward both rear and front doors, she licked her dry lips. "So, that means the elders may also stop in to speak with Caleb."

Leora shook her head, raising her hands. "*Nee*! I don't know! That depends on what they talk to my *daed* about. I'm just telling you so you know what has been happening. That, if the elders persuade my *daed* to stop beating and bullying *mamm*, he may actually back down. I don't know. All I know is that his behaviors and his attitudes have been. . . sexist. I mean, what would happen if he were to die some time? How would *mamm* support herself? He doesn't think about that."

Annie needed time to think. "Leora, let's go for a walk, you, Naomi and me, at lunch time. We'll tell Rebecca and Miriam that we're talking about. . . oh, about something else and we'll be back before it's time to re-open after lunch. I'm not mad at you. You just surprised me. *Gott* knows, I want this to stop. Wayne hasn't hit me, but he has raised his fist to me. . . meaning he felt the impulse."

Not wanting to rattle Annie again, Leora filed her thought in her mind so she could bring it up on their walk later. If Mr. Miller hears about the elders' visit to my *daed*, he may decide to back down. I wonder if there are any resources for us if we are hit by our husbands or boyfriends? "Okay, Annie. Denki. I just don't like how my *daed*, your husband. . . or any other men here sometimes treat their wives and daughters. It's wrong. We are just as capable as they are."

Annie stifled the impulse to sniffle and cry. Swallowing hard, she smiled, running her hand through the hair made visible by her head covering. "Denki. I am so grateful to *Gott* that you and Naomi are such good friends!" She turned her head as Naomi, Rebecca and Miriam came into the store, chattering all the while.

"Girls! I want to have a short meeting before we open up. Come!" Walking toward the back of the store, Annie arranged five chairs just behind the cashier's counter. "I want to see the front window, so we'll talk here. Now." Looking at her notes, Annie continued. "Our promotional sale went very well. Between last Tuesday and this Saturday, we sold progressively more and more quilts so that, by Saturday, we doubled our normal Saturday sales!"

She waited until the squeals and cries of "Wunderbaar!"

died down. "This means that, if things continue in this way, I may be able to give each of you raises early next year. But I don't want to count the chickens before their eggs are laid. So, let's just plan on working as hard as we have been doing. Naomi and I will work on more promotion ideas and we will have additional sales between now and the end of this year. Ideas?"

Naomi looked around. She already had a few, but she wanted to give the other girls a chance to weigh in. She smiled as Miriam raised her hand.

"How about an end-of-school promotion? We could focus on the lightweight, summery quilts."

Annie jotted the idea down, nodding her head.

Leora tossed her idea in: "I'm thinking that, with Wedding Season at the end of the harvest, we can offer wedding quilts and quilts in general for people wanting to give them as gifts."

Annie liked that idea, putting a small star next to her handwriting.

Rebecca was the last to weigh in. "I know we focus more on His birth at Christmas, but why not have a Christmas sale? I know my own *mamm* gets very busy in the months and weeks before Christmas and she doesn't always have time to work on finishing the quilts she wants to give to others."

Annie gazed into the far distance, thinking. "*Ja*, I like that. Because Wedding Season and Christmas—and Thanksgiving, for that matter—are so close together, it is difficult for us to spend much time in our quilting rooms. If we focus more on taking some of the stress off the mothers and wives and less on the 'sale' aspect, we should be okay. Although I do want to speak to Deacon Hannes and get his input first. Okay, I see people starting to wait outside. It's about that time, so let's open up. Remember, customer service with a smile! Oh, Leora and Naomi, let's go for a short walk during lunch. I want to refine some of these ideas a little. Rebecca, Miriam, would you please stay here and keep an eye on the shop while we're gone?" Standing, she hurried to the door and unlocked it.

"*Ja*, we'll be happy to," Miriam said as she smiled.

The morning was busy for the quilt shop. While it wasn't as busy as it had been the previous Saturday, everyone still moved quickly from customer to customer, explaining various quilting designs, then ringing up sales.

***

Caleb waited impatiently at the side of the store, looking for Wayne Lapp. The other man had asked for the meeting so he could offer suggestions for getting Annie to close her blamed quilt shop. "Well, there you are! I'm a busy man and my crops won't wait."

"C'mon, I'm sorry. I had to shake Lizzie off my trail because she knew I didn't have plans to come into town. Sometimes, it was easier when she was working. But it violated the natural, God-given order of things. That's why I ordered her to quit her job at your wife's shop. And that's what I want to discuss with you now. What I did to get Lizzie to quit. You have time for some coffee?"

Caleb gazed at the sun's position. If he didn't linger too long, he should be okay, he thought. "*Ja*, sure. Long as it doesn't take too long. Let's go to that English diner on the edge of Peace Valley."

"*Ja*, I know the one. I've stopped patronizing the little restaurant here. It's run by Mrs. Zook, Miriam's *mamm*. Her husband should talk to her and make her close it. He's a farmer. He makes enough to support all of them."

Caleb nodded, though something about Wayne's last statement rankled him. "'Woman-owned.' Two of the most unnatural words in the English vocabulary. If her husband owned it, that would be correct."

Wayne grinned at his friend. "True. But Tim Zook is one of them new-thinking men, believing that it's just peachy for his wife to own her own business. I know it's not in the *Ordnung*, but it should be—that only the husbands should own and work the businesses here in Peace Valley." By now, they had gotten to the diner. Escorted to a booth by a male server, they ordered coffee and slices of pie. "Now, this is what I did. . ." Looking around, he verified that nobody would overhear what he was telling Caleb. "My wife was real resistant to quitting her job as the assistant manager. So, I. . . convinced her. With a beating."

CHAPTER FIVE

Caleb had just taken a sip of hot coffee. Inhaling at his shock, he choked painfully as the brew burned. Coughing and spewing coffee over the table, he shook his head. "Warn a man, wouldn't you?"

Coughing a few more times, Caleb swiped at his streaming eyes with the back of his weathered hand. He repeated Wayne's furtive gesture, looking around. "You mean you raised your hands against your own wife? You do know that violates the *Ordnung*, no?"

Wayne flushed with irritation. Sitting back, he pondered leaving, then he decided he needed the support more. He chose to glare at Caleb instead. "Hey, you want help or to see your wife continuing to work?"

Caleb's mouth opened and closed twice as he decided he wanted the help. "The help. But go easy on your wife! Remember, they do still have roles in our community. Doesn't

Lizzie still make quilts at home, then sell them?"

"*Ja*, but that's from home. That don't violate the *Ordnung*. *Ja*, the money comes in real handy, but I don't want her working outside our home! She saw the wisdom of my decision real quick. That's what I'm suggesting to you. *Ja*, your wife owns her business, but it's diminishing you and your role in your family. It's also diminishing your role in Peace Valley. She could own her own home-based business and she should be just happy with that. Lizzie's perfectly happy making quilts at home, even though she cries and moans about wanting to help Barbara, her husband and newest baby."

"What's happening with them? I knew they had a new little one. She sick or what?"

"*Ja*. The English doctor diagnosed her with asthma and loaded her *mamm* up with medicines and some machine called a 'nebulizer.' Because the baby's so young, she doesn't know how to breathe in the medicine from an inhaler, so Barbara has to pour liquid medicine into a little cup and attach that to the nebulizer. It works by making the medicine into a mist. The baby wears a small, I don't know, mask over her mouth and nose so the medicine gets into her lungs."

Caleb scratched his cheek. "Ain't all that stuff expensive? Barbara doesn't work, right? So they rely on her husband's income? How are they affording all that?"

Here, Wayne shifted, feeling vaguely uncomfortable. "*Ja*. It is. And Lizzie was whining about needing to go back to work at the shop so she could help them with the baby's medicines. I stopped all that real fast."

Despite his misgivings, Caleb was curious. "How?"

Caleb glanced around again. He was grateful that he'd chosen a table closer to the kitchen. "Just before she finally saw the light and quit her job, I administered a 'reminder' to her. I knocked her around a little. That week, she took a resignation letter in to Annie and now, she's staying at home. When Barbara came to us about the medicine and Lizzie started making noise about wanting to go back to work, I just stood over her. . . you know how little she is. . . and I just raised one fist at her. She knew what I meant and she backed down." Remembering that morning and the night he'd beat Lizzie, Wayne's grin became predatory and somehow, frightening.

Caleb, seeing this, leaned back. He regretting eating his pie so quickly—now, his stomach was squirming just as though he had eaten a passel of snakes. Smothering a groan, he looked again at Wayne. "Okay. Suppose I did what you suggest. What's to say that Annie. . . or even Naomi, won't go to the elders with that?"

"That's when you let them know that what happens behind the front door of your house stays right there. You worried about the money?"

Caleb raised one shoulder in a slight shrug. Any more movement, and he was afraid he'd toss his pie all over the table. "*Mebbe*. Farming's not a sure science. The weather gets strange and there go the crops for a full season."

Wayne grunted in sympathy. "*Ja*, I know. I get an unreliable or dishonest customer and I can kiss a good sum of money goodbye. That's why I decided to. . . 'allow' Lizzie to make quilts from home and take them to your wife's shop. She gets a portion of the sale from each quilt. And *ja*, she is able to help with the baby's medicines."

Swallowing a little more of his coffee, Caleb shifted in his seat. "So. . . raise my hands against my wife. That'll work? What about if I just do what you did last time? Stand over her and raise my fists as though I'm going to hit her?"

"Caleb, you have to be ready to take every step possible! That's the only way. . . shhh." Taking a gulp of his coffee, Wayne shifted to a different topic. "So, the customer told me I had done a bad job with the headboard and dresser. He threatened not to pay me. It took me and my shop foreman to remind him that we had made everything exactly to his specifications." Glancing around with his eyes, Wayne assured himself that the server was now gone.

"If you're going to be successful in forcing Annie to sell the shop and stay at home, you have to hit her. Try not to bruise her too much, although that's not always possible. After the beating is over, apologize and just tell her that it's the stress that made you do that. Remind her how much you love her. . . then have the idea of, if she wants to work, she can work from home. And only from home. If she needs any reminders, just stand over her. She's tall, I know, but she's slender, ain't?"

Caleb nodded. "*Ja*. She is. I'm stronger than she is. It might work." Grimacing, he sighed, forcing back sudden nausea. "Okay. Next time it comes up, she gets a beating." Looking outside, Caleb saw that the shadows had shifted. "And now, I really got to get home." Pulling a few bills out of his wallet, he tossed them on the table. "Denki and I'll be seeing you."

Forcing himself to stand straight, Caleb strode outside and made a beeline for his buggy. The entire time he walked, his mind kept playing with him. And his stomach kept getting more and more messed up. His fists connecting with his wife's lovely face. The bruises and cuts on her face and body. Annie, crying and moaning.

By the time he got back to his buggy, the images had nauseated him completely. He had climbed to the seat and was ready to signal his horses to head back home, but his stomach had had enough. Leaning over the side, he lost his snack. The discussion with Wayne was so upsetting that he was sick two more times before finally pulling into the barn at home. I need medicine. Walking into the house, he looked around. Empty. As always.

In the bathroom, he swallowed medication intended to calm his stomach. Downstairs, he sat on the dark-blue sofa and leaned his head back on the sofa's back, willing his stomach to behave. A few minutes later, groaning, he ran into the downstairs bathroom and vomited again. *Nee*, no way can I eat lunch. But maybe I can turn this into a situation that works for me. I'll just rest for a while, then go to the barn. Caleb worked through his idea slowly, mindful of his tender stomach. When they come home tonight and see that I'm sick, I can say that the leftovers went bad. And I can start using that as a reason for her to sell the shop. Caleb gave a slight grin, then closed his eyes. I'll just rest for a few minutes, allow the medicine to do its work.

***

While Caleb was suffering the aftereffects of his meeting with Wayne, Annie, Naomi and Leora were walking slowly down the street, discussing what Annie and Leora had talked about earlier.

". . . And Leora told me that what her *daed* and your *daed* are doing is sexist. I was thinking, while we were between customers, that our community's *Ordnung* does allow us to work outside the home. We're not as conservative as the Old Order Amish, right? So your *daed* and your *daed* are behind the times. It's going to take us some time to convince them of that. Naomi, try to think of ways to remind your *daed* that my business has helped our family to keep our heads above water when crops have not grown as they should have, or when they have failed outright. I want you and Leora to study this sexism thing more closely so we can develop more defenses against what the men try to tell us. Me? I will go and talk to Lovina King, Hannes' wife. We are friends and I am thinking that I could get some valuable information about violations of our *Ordnung*. It may be that what your *daed* did violated the *Ordnung*. . ."

RACHEL STOLTZFUS

CHAPTER SIX

Here, Leora jumped in. "Annie, it is! Vernon told me that. That's why the elders are going to talk to my *daed* today. His *daed* won't be one of them, because Vernon talked to him. Once the elders talk to him, they'll have a better idea of whether he's going to comply with the *Ordnung* or whether they have to promise the *Meidung* to him. I'll try to get information from Vernon and let you know what happens. Do you want me to talk to him about what your husband is doing?"

Annie shook her head. "*Nee*. Not yet. I'm praying that Wayne will tell Caleb what happened and that will make them stop their behaviors. If need be, I can talk to Lovina and ask her to tell Hannes what is happening. It's time to get back to the shop. Remember, learn as much as you can about sexism so we can develop a plan."

***

Arriving home that night, Annie was surprised when she opened the refrigerator and saw that Caleb hadn't eaten any of the dinner she'd made for him.

"*Mamm*! Bring the cleaners with you, please! *Daed* was sick earlier and he didn't clean it up. Ewww." Naomi gulped back her own nausea and backed out of the first-floor bathroom.

Grabbing the needed cleaners, plus a pair of cleaning gloves, Annie hurried to the bathroom. "Oh, my! No wonder he didn't eat this afternoon. Go. Outside and get fresh air so you don't get sick."

Naomi obeyed instantly, running to the back door, where she inhaled deep breaths of fresh air. Sighing, she closed her eyes in relief—the nausea was subsiding.

Annie quickly cleaned up the bathroom, erasing all signs of Caleb's illness. After putting the cleaners, gloves and soiled cloths away, she hurried to the barn. "Do you feel better, Naomi?"

"Much. Denki. I'll stay out here for a little while more."

"*Gut.* I'm going to the barn to see if I find your *daed* and see what's wrong with him." Hurrying, Annie nearly ran to the barn. "Caleb? There you are! What happened to you? You were sick—I just cleaned it up."

"Up or downstairs?" By now, Caleb had built up a head of steam, justifying what he was about to do. His nausea had long since departed.

"Upstairs, too? I'll clean that up right away. Did you pick up a bug?" Annie was concerned. Money was already tight and they didn't need for Caleb to be laid up until he got well.

"Wife, I got sick from the food you stored in the refrigerator for me! While you should be at home, you're in that infernal store of yours, chatting and gossiping with the other wives and your. . . workers instead of being at home, cleaning and making our meals fresh! I felt this sickness building last night with stomach cramps. Even though I took antacids, it kept growing inside my stomach, until this morning, when I got horribly sick. *Nee*, I didn't eat what you left. I couldn't! And now that I have finally gotten all that poison out of my system, I am fairly starving! I want you to close that store, sell it, whatever you need to do. Soon!"

By now, Caleb was physically looming over Annie, who had backed up against the wide counter inside the barn. He raised one arm, hand fisted, implying that, if she didn't agree, he would strike her.

Annie, seeing Caleb's raised fist, gasped with fear. Seeing a slight opening between his body and the counter, she edged out as fast as she could, then, without giving him an answer, she ran out of the barn and back toward the house.

Naomi heard her *daed* yelling at her *mamm*. Running toward the barn, she ran headlong into her *mamm*, who was white-faced and fighting tears. "*Mamm*! What happened?"

Annie didn't speak. Instead, she gripped Naomi's arm,

pulling her toward the kitchen. In the house, she caught her breath and wiped away tears. "Your *daed* threatened me. Said that the food I put away for him went bad and made him sick. We'll make supper, then you will go to oh, either Leora's or the King's house. Let them know what just happened."

"*Mamm*, I'd better go to talk to Deacon King. If I go to Leora's, her *daed* will know what is up. And that we were the ones who alerted the deacon through Vernon."

Annie, her thoughts still scattered, nodded, realizing Naomi was right. "Okay. Just be back before bedtime. That's all I ask. I need to clean the upstairs bathroom. *Daed* was sick up there as well."

Gathering the cleaning items once more, Annie went upstairs. Holding her breath against the foul stench, she cleaned, still feeling shaky. Once the bathroom was cleaned, she threw the soiled cloths into the wash room and washed her hands before starting supper.

Caleb came silently into the kitchen, feeling somewhat ashamed of his outburst in the barn. Not liking the feeling, he scowled. "Well? Did you give thought to my ultimatum?"

Annie drew in a shaky breath. Not wanting to show fear, she stood tall and straight. "*Ja*. I did. It's not going to be easy to sell the shop in this economic downturn. Naomi, please stay. You need to know what goes into the thinking and planning." Feeling her thoughts coalescing around a theme, Annie felt more calm. "Caleb. I'm not buying medication or medical equipment for a seriously ill child. But I am employing five other young women here, one of them your daughter. To sell the shop, I would have to spend valuable funds on advertising. Hire an English attorney to draw up paperwork and pay more money to him. Find a buyer and pay even more money to run a credit check on them. Your crops are doing well—this year, thank *Gott*. But, what happens if a drought develops next year? Eventually, Naomi will get married and we need to save money for that. We're still paying off the loan to the bank for the equipment you had to replace. We also pay your employees. I'm not going to say no about selling, but I am telling you we have to think very carefully about how I would do this."

Caleb's scowl slowly lessened. "So, you aren't saying no? Just that we need to take some time?"

Annie's heart squeezed as she nodded. She didn't like to tell lies. "If you feel better, supper is ready."

"*Ja*. I do. Denki."

Supper was a quiet, strained meal that night. The usual talk and laughter that accompanied their meals was absent.

"*Mamm? Daed?* Do you mind if I go to visit with Leora? She asked me to stop by after cleaning up from supper. She wants to talk to me about one of our friends and some troubles she having." Twisting her fingers painfully, Naomi sent up a silent apology for her own lies.

Annie pretended to be upset. "Tonight? Why didn't you talk

on our lunch break?"

"*Mamm*, it's because the other girls were there. We couldn't exactly talk about our friend in front of them, could we?"

Sighing, Annie relented. "Okay, *ja*. As long as you are back before it gets full dark. It's summer, but I don't want you out after dark. Do you understand?"

"*Ja*, denki!"

"Daughter, I'm happy to see you trying to help your friends, but I do agree with your *mamm*. I don't like you traipsing all over the place, so be back before the moon comes up."

"Denki, *daed*. I will." Grabbing the cloth, Naomi cleaned the kitchen as Annie washed dishes, then she helped her *mamm* dry and put them away.

***

Riding to Vernon's house, Naomi breathed deeply, willing her heart rate to fall back to normal. On the way, she sent a fervent prayer to *Gott*, asking him to open her *daed*'s heart to the reality that her *mamm* needed to work. When she arrived at Vernon's, she gulped back a sob. Knocking on the door, she waited, nerves causing her to wring her hands.

"Naomi! Come in! This is a wunderbaar. . . Naomi? What's wrong?" Vernon was very familiar with her expressions and he knew she was frightened right now.

Naomi dragged in a large breath, willing herself to stay calm. "Vernon, is your *daed* here? And your *mamm*?"

"*Ja,* they are. Come into the kitchen." Vernon curled his hand around Naomi's upper arm, trying to give her comfort. "*Daed, mamm*? Naomi's here. I think. . . something happened at her house. She asked to speak with you. Naomi do you want me to stay or leave?"

"Oh, please stay! I need you to know this as well." Naomi grabbed Vernon's hand in both of her own as she begged for his presence.

"Come, Naomi. Sit. Would you like some water or lemonade? It appears you don't need coffee right now." Deacon Hannes King's kind brown eyes took in Naomi's upset. He was sure he knew what it was about, but knew that Naomi needed to say what happened.

"Lemonade, please. Denki, Mrs. King." She took a gulp of the tart beverage before sinking into a chair. Closing her eyes, she saw the frightening scene outside the barn, which caused her to shudder. "Deacon, thank you for seeing me so unexpectedly. My *mamm* knows I'm here, but my *daed* thinks I'm at my friend's house. I know the other elders are meeting with Mr. Lapp this evening. *Mamm* said she saw *daed* walking down the street with Mr. Lapp a few days ago. We're concerned that Mr. Lapp is giving *daed* ideas and suggestions about how to make *mamm* quit her quilt store.

"Well, this afternoon, we got home at our usual time so we

could make supper. Only *daed* had been sick, so *mamm* cleaned that up, then she went to the barn when she couldn't find him in the house. He got so mad at her, deacon!" Naomi sniffled, trying to hold tears back. Wiping her cheeks, she continued. "He blamed her for his sickness today, saying that the food she had prepared for his dinner earlier in the week was bad. He accused her of giving him food poisoning. I heard him yelling at her and ran to the barn. Deacon, I saw. . . I saw. . ."

Here, Naomi had to stop. Her sobs were too strong. Lovina and Hannes King took her hands, helping her to calm down. Naomi finally calmed down enough to continue. "I'm sorry. I saw. . . my *daed* trapping *mamm* between his body and the work shelf in the barn. He had one arm raised like this. . ." Here, Naomi imitated a man about to strike someone else. "His hand was in a fist."

Lovina looked at Hannes, silently communicating to him.

Hannes caught the message and nodded. "Naomi, you were brave to come here and tell us what you saw today. *Ja*, the elders are talking to Mr. Lapp at this moment, offering him help and reminding him that, if he continues to threaten his wife—or his daughter—in this way, he faces the *Meidung*. I am thinking we need to go and visit with your *daed* to give him the same message. "

Lovina began speaking when her husband finished. "Naomi, I don't know if you're aware of this, but we do have some families here who are willing to help families struggling with domestic violence. The English communities frown on this kind of treatment of men's wives. I'm also aware that some English wives actually physically abuse their husbands. We don't want or need any of that kind of treatment here, so Vernon's *daed* and I have been working with some of the volunteer couples. I would like to introduce you and your *mamm* to one of them. They have agreed to work with families in need of attention, prayer and. . . well, if you want to call it that, 'retraining' in handling disagreements in a loving, safe way. I want you to tell your *mamm* all of this because she and your *daed* would have to agree to this work. If Hannes, along with other elders, visit with your *daed* and let him know they are aware of what happened today, they will remind him of what he is risking if he refuses."

Naomi listened closely. "*Ja*. I can talk to her while we're on the way to the shop tomorrow. Mrs. King, do you and your husband know what 'sexism' is?" Naomi had recovered her usual calm and presence of mind so that she was not afraid of bringing up this topic.

Lovina nodded. "I do. Hannes and I have no doubt that what is happening between your *mamm* and *daed*, as well as the Lapps, is because of sexism, when one gender believes it is superior to the other gender. Now, do you mind telling me something?"

Naomi nodded. "Okay. What?"

"Well, tell me two things, please. First, what is Mr. Lapp

trying to get your *daed* to do? And second, why did your *daed* threaten your *mamm* today?"

Naomi sighed. "We think Mr. Lapp is explaining to *daed* how he forced his wife to quit her job at the quilt shop. I mean, it's not like the two of them have been the best of friends before. I've seen them together at least twice and *mamm* saw them this week."

Vernon was angry that anyone could think he was superior to anyone of the other gender. Needing to walk off some of his anger, he gestured to Naomi and his parents that he would be back in a few minutes. "I'm just so upset at all of this. I need to walk it off."

"That's fine. Just don't be too long." Hannes sent a stern look to his youngest son.

"I won't. Naomi, I promise, I'll be back in soon." Vernon tried to smile.

Naomi nodded. Seeing the effects of her story on him worried her. "Vernon, I'm okay. I just hope we can get help for the Lapps, my *daed* and my *mamm*. After Vernon had walked out the back door, Naomi continued. "We believe that Mr. Lapp is trying to get my *daed* to attack my *mamm* physically. *Mamm* remembers that, shortly before she quit, Mrs. Lapp came into work with a huge bruise on her face. She tried to explain it away, but my *mamm* wasn't fooled. Mrs. Lapp finally admitted that her husband beat her up. Leora remembers the beating as well. And, this is what *mamm* and I have been talking about so much. *Daed* is trying to force *mamm* to give up and sell her quilting shop. But *mamm* doesn't want to. Her shop employs four of us. Five if she's able to find an assistant manager. He tells her that women belong at home, cleaning, cooking and taking care of the children.

"Tonight, *mamm* reminded him that her store allows women who make their quilts at home to sell them through the store and earn some money. I. . . I hope I'm not betraying any confidences here, but Mrs. Lapp has begun to take her quilts into the shop. Because her newest grandchild has been diagnosed with asthma. And her medicines and that special machine are so expensive. So, that's what Mrs. Lapp is doing with the money she earns from selling her quilts at our store."

Hannes had heard enough. Getting up, he began to stride around the kitchen. "*Nee*, Naomi, don't worry. I'm feeling the same as Vernon—frustrated, angry." After a few minutes, he calmed down and Vernon came in at the same time. "Naomi, I got so frustrated because both your *daed* and Mr. Lapp are missing the importance of their wives' work outside the home. Our *Ordnung* has been modified, allowing married women to hold outside jobs. I don't know if you remember this, but didn't one of your *daed*'s crops almost fail a year or two ago, when we had that long drought?"

Naomi's mouth dropped open. She knew where the deacon was going with this! "*Ja*! It did and it was only *maam's* ownership of the shop that allowed us to keep going, get food on the table and keep paying the note at the bank for *daed*'s new equipment! *Mamm* and I talked about that because she wants me to be as aware of finances as possible."

"Wise woman." Lovina smiled. "Naomi, I think my husband wants the elders to use this reminder to show your *daed* that your *mamm* and her shop are valuable and precious to your family."

"My wife knows me well, Naomi." Hannes gave a small smile. That's exactly what I want to do. I will go see the other ministers and the bishop tomorrow and we will stop in to visit with your *daed* and *mamm* later this week."

Naomi experienced competing feelings. First, she felt absolute relief, then fear of what her *daed* would do or say.

Vernon watched as Naomi's face changed. "Naomi, don't worry. He won't do anything to you or your *mamm*. The elders will make it clear to him that, by threatening physical violence against your *mamm*, he violated our *Ordnung*. And that he is risking the ban."

Closing her eyes, Naomi forced herself to calm down. "Okay. I know that he doesn't want to go under the *Meidung*. Mrs. King, who are these families that are helping you?"

"I'm sure you're very familiar with one of them, as our son is dating Leora. You're also familiar with them. Eli and Lizzie Yoder."

Naomi smiled, her first genuine smile since coming into the house. "They are perfect! I like how they treat each other and their children. And they treat other families with kindness and respect."

"That doesn't mean they'll allow abusers to get away with their bad behaviors." Hannes raised one finger as a reminder. "If they hear or witness anything, they will report it to the elders, and they will require couples to commit to treating each other with respect."

Naomi felt more comfortable with the idea by the minute. Closing her eyes and sending up a brief prayer, she nodded. Opening her eyes, she spoke. "*Ja*. If this helps my parents to stop fighting about the shop and it keeps *daed* from harming *mamm*, then let's do it. Also, if *daed* would just open his blamed eyes and see that the shop has kept his farm from failing in rough years so he stops bothering *mamm* about closing or selling the shop."

Hannes smiled at Naomi as he realized she was very intelligent. "Those are excellent goals and definitely reachable. Don't tell your *mamm* this until tomorrow. I would like to stop at your house tomorrow, at the earliest, but that depends on the other elders' schedules."

"I need to get home. I promised both *mamm* and *daed* I'd be home by the time it got dark and it's close to that now. Denki!" Standing, she got ready to leave the house.

"Let me follow you, please. Just to the end of your lane so I know you got home safely." Vernon didn't like the idea of her driving late at night.

"*Ja*, that's fine." Naomi walked out with Vernon and waited as he checked to make sure the horses were properly hitched to the buggy. Settling on the seat, she waited as he led his own team out of the barn.

"You go ahead and I'll follow." Vernon waited for Naomi to signal her horses to move.

On her way home, Naomi thought about everything she had discussed with the Kings. Knowing that another Amish couple could help her parents correct their relationship's course was a huge relief to her. Feeling better and better by the minute, she gave Vernon a genuine smile as she turned onto her lane.

"I'll see you on Friday!" Vernon said, just loud enough for her to hear.

"That sounds *gut*! See you then!" Hurrying the rest of the way, Naomi was relieved that the sun hadn't yet fully set. Pulling into the barn, she was surprised to see her *daed* working at his worktable. "Hi, *daed*! Are you feeling okay?"

"*Ja*, daughter. I'm better, denki. How was your visit with Leora?"

"*Gut*. We talked about quilt patterns we want to try, as well as our plans for the weekend." Naomi had already come up with things she and Leora had already talked about so she wouldn't really be lying.

"Plans for the weekend? You mean with Vernon and Jethro? Hmmm, as long as your work here is done. And, if you insist on working at the shop, that's not going to give you much time. Weeding? Cleaning the house?"

Naomi knew what her *daed* was doing. "*Daed, mamm* and I got the cleaning done earlier this week, when the shop was closed. And I got the weeding done in the morning, before it got too hot."

Caleb knew he'd been outsmarted by his own daughter. This didn't improve his mood. His voice settling into a low growl, he pointed at her. "Daughter, you'd better make very sure that all of your work here has been done. I am still your *daed* and I still have authority over you."

Naomi's mouth dropped open. "*Ja, daed*, I know. I was just letting you know that I got all of my chores done already. I also checked the garden again and ensured that there are no weeds there."

Annie came into the barn as Naomi finished speaking to her *daed*. "Caleb? What's wrong?" She sent a frown to Naomi, along with a silent message in her eyes.

"She was sassing me and I was reminding her that I still hold authority over her. She told me that she, Leora and their boyfriends have already made plans for this weekend. And I reminded her that she needs to finish her work here first."

"Naomi, you know our rules here at home. Work first, pleasure last. If your work is truly done, then yes, you can spend time with your friends. But if it isn't, you'll need to make adjustments and let them know. Do you understand?"

"*Ja, mamm*. I'm sorry, *daed*. I didn't intend to come across like I was sassing you. *Mamm*, my work is done. I'll. . . I'll get supper started."

"*Nee*, daughter. I have that underway. I need your help with the biscuits and dessert, and, when you're done with that, look through our work calendar for this month to make sure we have everything ready for tomorrow and next week."

"*Ja, mamm*." Naomi made her voice meek and quiet. Lowering her head, she tried to give the impression that she was disappointed with herself as she went to the house. Pulling the ingredients out for the apple crisp, she thought about what her *mamm* may have been trying to tell her. She overheard her *daed* talking to her *mamm*.

"Annie, I still have a few things left to do. The new boy is still slow at his work, so it's up to me to get it done."

"Ach! How long has he worked for you?" Annie was sympathetic.

"Only for a few weeks. I'm giving him another three, maybe four weeks before I decide whether he stays or goes. I'll be in by the time you put supper on the stove."

"Okay." Annie hurried back to the house. Inside, she checked Naomi's progress on the apple crisp and biscuits. "Naomi, you handled that well. Have you decided whether you're comfortable moving into the manager's position?"

"*Ja*, I think I can handle it. When are you going to make the announcement?" Annie finished peeling the apples and began mixing the crisp as she watched the outdoors, looking for her *daed*.

"I'll bring it up tomorrow afternoon, after we get home. What I want to do is spend mornings only at the shop."

CHAPTER SEVEN

Naomi's hands stilled in their work. "You mean I would be responsible for everything in the afternoons? Including counting out the day's sales and making the deposit?"

"Exactly. But I want to bring this up with you as though we had never discussed it, understand?"

Naomi understood perfectly. "I like your ideas. Discussing them in front of *daed* will take some of the pressure off of you."

"That's my hope and prayer, daughter. I hope he will see that I am serious about making a good home for him and you while keeping ownership of the store."

Naomi gave a quick look out the window. "*Mamm*, I think he wants you home full time, with no shop at all."

"*Ja*, that's what he says. Deep down though, he knows that my little shop has saved our family and farm when conditions have made it impossible for him to have a good harvest. I hope that, when you go out with your friends tomorrow after I break my news and inform you that you're the new manager, that he will want to talk with me."

"*Mamm*, but I think it's safer to have that discussion while I'm around! What if he gets mad at you and. . ."

"There's a repeat of what you saw in the barn?" Annie continued stirring the vegetables as she considered Naomi's point. "Good point. Then you verify your plans for tomorrow with the others and let me know while we're on the way to the shop."

Naomi sighed. "*Ja*, that's better." Putting the biscuits into the hot oven, she indicated the back yard. "*Daed*'s coming in."

Annie nodded. Moving to the salad, she broke up a head of lettuce and began cutting up a tomato. "Naomi, is the crisp almost ready?"

"*Ja*, I'm about to put it in with the biscuits." Naomi's head swiveled around as she heard Caleb scraping dirt from his shoes. "Hi, *daed*! Supper will be ready in a little while!"

"*Gut*. I am powerful hungry, daughter. What did you and your *mamm* make tonight?"

Annie answered. "Fried chicken, baked potatoes with the fixings, salad and mixed vegetables. Naomi made the biscuits and some apple crisp."

Caleb closed his eyes in anticipation. "You two made my

favorite meal! Denki!"

Annie and Naomi smiled at each other. As they did so, Naomi wondered if her *mamm* had planned this particular meal on purpose.

After dinner was over and Caleb was nursing a fresh cup of coffee, Naomi rose from the table. "*Mamm*, I'll clean the kitchen and do the dishes."

"And I'll dry. Thank you." By the time Caleb had finished his last cup of coffee, leaving the kitchen, Annie was ready to clean the table.

"I'm going to get ready now. Jethro should be here before long and I want to comb my hair and put on a fresh head covering."

"Okay. Just do not be too late. Understand?" Annie motioned toward the living room with her eyes.

"Okay. I'll let Jethro know I need to be home early." In her room, Naomi considered everything her *mamm* was doing. Fried chicken and telling me to be in early. She's trying to soften *daed* up! Given how he's been treating her, I think she's right to do so. If we can get him to stay in a happier mood, he might eventually give in about her store.

Finishing her hair and setting a fresh head covering on her head, she hurried downstairs. A few seconds later, Jethro knocked at the back door. "*Daed, mamm*, I'll be back early. I promise!" Naomi hurried out before her *daed* could say anything. "Jethro, I need to be back in earlier than usual. We're trying not to upset *daed*."

"Why would he be upset about us going out?" Jethro's forehead crinkled in confusion.

"He's been trying to make the point that, if I'm not at home, I can't get my chores done. I have some news for you when we meet up with Leora and Vernon. Where are we going, by the way?"

"We thought we would take you two over to the new coffee shop, enjoy some coffee and sweets."

"I hope I can make room! *Mamm* made fried chicken tonight!"

"Mmm, one of my favorites!"

Naomi giggled. "I'll make sure to get the recipe from *mamm*."

***

In the coffee shop, Naomi and Jethro sat down with Leora and Vernon. "I want to try one of these new coffees," said Leora.

"Me, too! Which one?"

"Let's look at the menu to see which would be best." Leora's eyes twinkled as she read through the small menu.

After both couples had placed their orders, they waited and talked. "Leora, *mamm* has news for me. She's going to break it to me in front of *daed* tomorrow after work."

Leora's eyes widened. "I think I know! But tell us!"

Naomi waited for a split second before she spoke. "She asked me to think about moving up to the manager's position. There's a couple reasons for this. I'm happy and I'm saying yes. *Mamm* and I are hoping and praying that, by my becoming manager, she'll be able to spend more time at home, where *daed* wants her. That, by spending more time at home, he'll stop with his demands that she sell the shop and stop working outside our home."

Leora became serious. "I pray that will be so. *Daed* is still very firm that *mamm* has to stay at home. He's only okay with her selling quilts on consignment because of my niece's health problems and the costs of her medications."

"Leora, has he stopped. . . physically threatening your *mamm*?" Naomi was tense, feeling her entire body beginning to tighten up.

"*Ja*, especially after the elders came by the other night."

Jethro leaned in toward Leora. "Can you tell us what happened? Or is that confidential?"

"Only because we know what's been. . ." Leora gasped as several coffee mugs went crashing to the ground. Along with her gasp, the others jumped as well. ". . . Going on. The bishop and two ministers came to the house and took *daed* outside. I tried to stick as close to the kitchen door as I could without being caught. They told him that they had been informed that he had attacked *mamm* a few months ago, leaving bruises on her face. He couldn't deny it, but he did try to defend himself with the *Ordnung* of all things."

Vernon let out a bark of laughter. "How? Physically assaulting someone else is a violation, period!"

"He tried to say that *mamm* was violating the *Ordnung* by working outside the house at all. He tried to say that, if she hadn't begun working at the quilt shop, he wouldn't have been forced to exert his husbandly right to discipline her. The elders were having none of that. They reminded him that our *Ordnung*, in its current form, does allow married and unmarried women to work outside the home so they can provide for the economic needs of their families. So, Naomi, if your own *daed* tries to say that your *mamm* is violating the *Ordnung*, she can tell him that he's wrong."

Vernon cleared his throat. "Speaking of which, Naomi. The elders are going to go and see your *daed* tomorrow after breakfast. I hope you and your *mamm* will either be away from home or working on chores."

Naomi felt chilled at the thought that her own *daed* would soon be confronted by the elders. Shivering, she picked up her cup of coffee and took a large gulp. "We'll be going to work. Saturday's a short day and *mamm* wants to make the announcement of my promotion to the others. Will the elders be speaking to my *mamm* as well?"

"I would think so. They spoke to Mrs. Lapp and she confirmed what happened and why it happened."

Naomi was troubled. "On one hand, I'm glad they'll be speaking to her, because she can tell them that she'll only be working at the shop half-time. On the other hand, she'll be at work and they won't be able to get her side of this mess."

"Ach, good point, Naomi. When I get home later on, I will let my *daed* know that so he can call the ministers and deacon. What time do you and your *mamm* usually leave for work?"

About eight-fifteen, more or less. That gives us time to make sure the store is presentable and put the till in the cash register. Also, it gives us a few minutes for a meeting so we all know what's happening."

"Okay." Vernon turned to a passing barista. "Excuse me, but do you have the time?"

"Sure!" He looked at his watch. "It's about nine-forty-five. We're closing in forty-five minutes."

"Denki." Looking at the others, Vernon pointed toward the door. "We should get home. Naomi can't be getting into trouble. And I'm sure Leora feels the same way."

The two couples left, climbing into the courting buggies and headed back to Peace Valley. Naomi was quiet, thinking of the coming meeting.

"You okay?" Jethro gave Naomi a worried look.

"*Ja*. I'm just thinking about the meeting tomorrow. If *mamm* hasn't gone to bed yet, I'll let her know that we should find a way of leaving a little later than usual. But if she's in bed. . ."

"Just wait until you're making breakfast?"

"*Ja*. While *daed* is feeding the livestock. I'm sure we can create a reason to leave a little bit later. Vernon said he would be telling his *daed* that they need to get here before we leave. . ."

"Vernon's smart. He'll work things out and tell his *daed* what time you leave, so that they are there well before your usual departure time."

Naomi relaxed a little at that. "*Ja*, that is true. Leora picked a good man, and so did I."

"Thank you! I need to ask you this before we get to your parent's house. What do you think of my *mamm* and *daed* helping your *daed* with his anger at your *mamm* working outside the house?"

"I like your parents. A lot. I like how they think. . .*ja*, I think it would be *gut* for them to work with my *daed* and *mamm*. She needs to know how to make him stop before he gets all riled."

"That is true. Okay, I'll tell them when I get home." After bringing Naomi to the front gate of the house, he leaned over and gave her a soft kiss, then drove the team into the yard, where he escorted Naomi to the front door. "I'll see you tomorrow evening?"

"*Ja*. You will. Good night!" Naomi smiled and waved at Jethro before walking into the house. Turning toward the kitchen, she prayed that her *mamm* was still up. In the kitchen, she sighed with relief. "*Mamm*, you're still up! Is everything okay?"

"*Ja*, just thinking of tomorrow."

"Me, too. Is *daed* already asleep?"

"Mmm-hmm. Long since. Why?"

"*Mamm*, Jethro, Leora and Vernon and I were talking about our family's situations." Here, she lowered her voice slightly. "The elders visited Mr. and Mrs. Lapp the other evening and got confirmation that Mr. Lapp assaulted Mrs. Lapp. And Vernon told me that the elders are going to be here tomorrow. They are going to want to talk to *daed* and you. Is there any way we can leave a little later than normal?"

"Did you tell them what time we leave?"

"Yes, I did. Jethro's sure that Vernon is telling his *daed* what time we leave so they can be here well before we have to go."

Annie exhaled a deep sigh and dropped her chin toward her chest. "Daughter, I am just so grateful to *Gott* right now! He is working all things for *gut* here. Your *daed* is going to find out that threatening me and trying to force me to sell the store violates the *Ordnung* and he is also going to find out that I am making you manager so I can spend more time here. Thank you, Lord!"

Both women paused at a creak in the hallway. Annie looked toward the stairs. In a normal tone of voice, she offered water to Naomi.

"*Ja*, just water. We had coffee drinks and snacks and I don't want to get too full to sleep comfortably."

Waiting a few seconds more, they assured themselves that the house was just settling. Caleb was still asleep.

"So, I will pray that they get here much closer to seven than eight-fifteen. I'll be making eggs, home-fried potatoes and sausage tomorrow morning. You make biscuits. As far as your *daed* knows, we won't know anything of the visit from the elders. We'll be getting ready to leave for work, period."

"Okay. I'd better get to bed. Morning is going to come. . ."

"Awfully quickly. Denki, daughter, for telling me about this." Annie hugged her daughter.

***

The next morning, the ministers gathered at the King home, which was closest to the Miller's home. "We need to get there *gut* and early. Mrs. Miller and her daughter usually leave home by eight-fifteen." The bishop looked at his ministers and the deacon. "I don't want this kind of thing threatening our families, so I want to make it very clear to Caleb that he has to stop threatening his wife and daughter. Are we ready?"

Climbing into the bishop's buggy, they set out for the Miller home. Pulling into the front yard and under a large, spreading tree, the elders jumped out of the buggy and walked up to the house. Knocking on the door, they waited.

Caleb answered the door. Seeing the four elders, his face paled and his eyes grew wide. "Bishop! I. . . hope nothing bad has happened."

"Caleb, I believe you know just why we are here. Come outside. We want to talk to you."

Caleb moved on legs that had lost all feeling. Collapsing onto the porch swing, he waited, knowing what was coming.

The bishop took the lead. "Caleb, we have had some sad and disturbing news. That you have been trying to force your wife to give up her ownership of Peace Valley Quilt Place so you can make her stay at home. Further, we got word that you have been meeting with Wayne Lapp to get additional ideas on how you can prevail upon Annie to make her quit and sell her store. Is this true?"

Caleb nodded with reluctance. "The *Ordnung*. . ."

"Says nothing about wives and older daughters about being required to stay at home. You are aware, aren't you, that, after the Great Recession of 2008, we changed our rules so that our wives and daughters could work outside the home? We view them as full partners in our marital relationships and in our homes. By trying to force Annie to sell her shop, you are violating the *Ordnung*."

Hannes King spoke up. "Further, we have been told that, just a few days ago, after meeting with Wayne Lapp, you raised your fist to your wife in the midst of an argument. Is this true?" As Hannes asked the question, his face and eyes communicated real sadness and disappointment.

It was these emotions, more than anything, that got to Caleb. Setting his mug down between his feet, he wrung his big, weathered hands together. "*Ja*. It is. I have always held the belief that the women are supposed to stay at home. Partners or not, they can contribute from the home." He refused to bend.

"If that is what they wish and what they are able to contribute, *ja*, this is true." One of the ministers sat forward, gazing into Caleb's face. "But, if the wife or daughters have a skill or specialized knowledge, they are encouraged—not 'allowed,' Caleb—encouraged to use those skills toward providing support for their families. As I understand it, your wife was able to attend vocational training, where she took business classes. My own wife contributes quilts to her shop and the money she gets paid has helped our household out when my crops haven't done well. Now, would you rather rely on your pride and have your family suffering after a crop failure? Or would you rather elevate Annie to a position next to you, where she can make a full contribution from her skills, interests and knowledge?"

The bishop leaned forward once again. "Caleb, you know full well why we are here. You have a decision to make. Repent and continue within our community. Or refuse to repent and face the ban. We are going to go in and speak with your wife now. If you would come in. . ."

RACHEL STOLTZFUS

CHAPTER EIGHT

Standing and grabbing his mug of now-cold coffee, Caleb let the elders into the house. "Annie! The elders want to talk to you. I'll be in the barn, working." Filling his mug with the last of the coffee, he walked out through the kitchen.

Annie and Naomi looked at each other, their eyes wide. "*Mamm*, you go talk to the ministers. I'll finish in here before we leave."

Sitting at the kitchen table with the four ministers, Annie verified everything. "*Ja*, he has been trying to force me to sell my shop so I can stay at home every day. I've been doing everything I can to make sure that everything here is done—providing meals for his dinner, cleaning the house on Mondays, when the store is closed. My daughter has consented to becoming the store manager, which will enable to me to work half-time so I can give Caleb a part of his wish."

"*Gut*! You have been trying to work with your husband on

this issue. You are aware that the *Ordnung*, as it is currently written, does allow you to work?" The bishop's gaze met Annie's face.

"*Ja*, bishop. I am. I want to work with Caleb on this. I don't want him getting angry at me and threatening to hit me. That's why I came up with the idea of promoting Naomi."

"*Gut*. He is thinking and praying over his options. He knows what they are. Before we go, I am going to go to the barn and let him know that you have been trying to work with him on keeping your store and giving him some of what he's been seeking. Does he know that Naomi is becoming manager?"

"*Nee*. She only made her decision yesterday and we haven't had the time to break the news to him."

"Then I will bring him back in here, unless you need to leave for the shop now?"

Annie checked the wall clock. "We still have some time before we have to go."

"I'll let myself out the back." The bishop hurried, knowing that time was vital. In the barn, he saw Caleb leaning over the work bench, his head lowered. "Caleb? Are you okay?"

"As okay as I'll ever be, *ja*. What is it?"

"I have a development that you may like, if you'll come back to the house." The bishop smiled with encouragement.

Caleb grabbed his coffee mug and swallowed the last of his

coffee. "What is it?"

"*Nee*, you need to hear this from Annie and Naomi. Come!"

Caleb swung the back door open and, after the bishop entered, left it open so a cool breeze could enter. "Annie, what is it?"

"Husband, would you please sit? I have news that I hope you might like." After Caleb took his usual seat at the head of the table, Annie took in a huge breath. Looking into her husband's deep, normally kind, brown eyes. "Husband, I asked Naomi to become the manager of the shop. She agreed to do so last night, but we didn't get the chance to tell you this then. She's going to work all day long at the store while I work half-days. I'll go in just after lunch and close with her. That way, I'll be here at home more as you wish me to be. But that also means that I will be able to continue contributing to our family's financial well-being."

Caleb nodded. This was, indeed a surprise! One he could be happy with. Knowing he couldn't push for more, he decided to accept the inevitable. But. . . "What about Naomi? What will happen if she and Jethro decide to get married after they are baptized?"

Naomi had been quiet the entire time, just watching and listening. "*Daed*, Jethro and I have talked about this already. We haven't yet made a firm decision on getting married because we are still too young. At least I am. But, he has told me that, if I still want to work at the shop or anywhere else within Peace Valley, he is fine with that. He knows that I can make some valuable contributions to our family, if we get married." Knowing her *daed*'s temper, Naomi forced herself to keep looking at his face. Her voice became more steady the longer she spoke.

"Before we leave." The bishop raised his hand. "I want to bring up one more thought and offer, then we need to let Annie and Naomi get to the shop. Caleb, Annie, what would you think about sitting down for some informal chats with Eli and Lizzie Yoder? While Lizzie has chosen to work from her home, she and Eli fully support the rights of women to work outside the home. They aren't going to look down at you for our having come to speak with you. They just want to see you grow from this situation and become a stronger couple and family."

Caleb had taken in a lot that morning and he still needed to get into the barn. Dropping his face into one hand, he sighed. "Bishop, I am going to back off on Annie and Naomi working in her shop. I repent of everything I did to her and Naomi. I. . . Annie, Naomi, I ask for your forgiveness. I apologize and I won't try to make you sell the shop. Naomi, congratulations. I know you have a *gut*, loving heart and you will do a wunderbaar job as manager. And, thank you for agreeing so that your *mamm* can spend more time here at home. Bishop, can Annie and I discuss the offer to work with the Yoders? I will have Naomi get a message to you through Jethro."

"That works out very well. I am happy to see that you repented, because we just want to see you, Annie and Naomi living in loving, supportive relationships. And now, I believe your wife and daughter should be getting to the store. Annie, my wife has a quilt just about ready for consignment. She will take it in to you next week sometime."

"*Gut*! I look forward to it. Caleb, we will be home by mid-afternoon. If you want, there are fried chicken, a baked potato and some vegetables for you."

"Denki, wife. I will heat them up and enjoy them."

***

At the shop, Annie and Naomi had a short meeting with Rebecca, Miriam and Leora. Before the meeting ended, Annie broke the news that Naomi was stepping up to the manager's position. After the flurry of congratulations and squeals had ended. Annie clapped her hands. "We need to open up! I already see tourists waiting! Let's make it a good, productive day!"

"*Ja*, this is the Giant Dahlia quilt, made by one of our best Peace Valley quilters. It would make a wonderful anniversary gift! If you are ready to buy now, I'm happy to wrap it up for you. Or, do you need more time. . ."

"Actually, the price is well within my budget. I'll take it now, thank you!" The English woman smiled with excitement as she imagined her daughter and son-in-law seeing the gift for the first time. Pulling out her credit card she handed it to Annie, who quickly rang up the sale.

"Rebecca, Miriam, would you please box up the Giant Dahlia for Mrs. Thompson?

"*Ja*, I am so excited this one sold! Mrs. King will be so happy." Miriam glowed as she spoke.

After closing the shop for lunch, Annie, Naomi and her employees discussed the day's events.

"Girls, I have decided to tell you what happened today. You are aware that I have been struggling with my husband's demands that I close the shop. Well, with Naomi's promotion, that is no longer a possibility. He has promised he isn't going to try to make me sell the shop. Rebecca, I have been thinking and praying about what happened to you. Naomi and Leora actually told me that they purposely chose the young men they are seeing. Have you gotten to that point yet?"

Rebecca nodded as she swallowed her lunch. "*Ja*. I decided to take some time from dating. I want to be comfortable with who I am and with what I have to offer to a future husband and to Peace Valley."

"*Gut*." This was Leora. "Take all the time you need. There are plenty of wunderbaar young men out there and someone is just waiting to be ready to meet and love you. Before you get into a dating relationship, try to find out how he feels, in the future, about his wife working outside the home. Contributing to the family's income."

Naomi jumped in. "We have a lot to offer to the young men

we date. Jethro knows this. If we decide to marry, he knows that I will be a full partner with him, standing next to him, not behind him. He works as a farrier, so he has plenty of work. But if he ever goes through a period where the work just isn't coming to him, he knows that my work here will help keep us from sinking under the bills. If we get married!" Naomi sent an impish look to her *mamm*.

On the way home after locking up the shop and making the bank deposit, Naomi and Annie talked. "*Mamm*, would you have any problem with my talking to Jethro's parents? I know *daed* is still trying to make up his mind, but I would like to find out, ahead of time, what the Yoders would say to him and you."

Annie considered. "*Nee*, I have no problem with that. Tomorrow's meeting Sunday, so why don't you see if you can speak to Mrs. Yoder at lunch?"

"I will, *mamm*, thanks."

At home, Caleb sat down with Annie and talked about the morning's visit. "Annie, I am truly sorry about my actions toward you. It will never happen again. I was thinking about the Yoder's offer and I am willing to sit down with them when they can come here. Or if they want us to go over to their house."

Annie, overwhelmed, put her hands over her mouth. "Caleb, denki. Naomi actually offered to speak to Mrs. Yoder after meeting tomorrow and find out what they would like to speak with you about."

Instead of getting mad, Caleb understood now that his wife and daughter were doing everything they could to make life easier for him. "Well. . . hmmm. *Ja.* Okay. That's fine. Aren't they the parents of the boy she's dating?"

Annie grimaced slightly, knowing that Caleb might be uncomfortable with that. "Well, *ja.* They are. Is that a problem?"

Caleb sighed. "Will they tell their son what we talk about?"

"Oh, Caleb, *Nee!* They will keep our meetings between the four of us. All I know is that Mrs. King knew that they could talk to us and keep everything within our district." She held her breath, knowing what her unspoken words said.

"Within our district. Meaning that, if I hadn't met with the elders and I had continued to try and make you give up the store, you may have called the police?"

"If it came to that. Or if I hadn't been able to, someone else would have."

Caleb's breath whooshed out in a long sigh. "I guess I should view their visit this morning as a blessing, then."

Annie refused to back down. "It would seem so, *ja.* Oh, Naomi will begin her first day as manager on Tuesday. I will begin training her on what she hasn't yet learned how to do. And I will be home a little bit after dinner time, Tuesday through Friday."

Caleb looked into Annie's eyes. "So, that means that Saturday will be the only full day you'll work?"

"*Ja*. I get home shortly after dinner and work on things here. Housework, cleaning, shopping, whatever needs doing."

"Annie, if I hadn't been such a stubborn old man and had just given you the room you needed, would you have come to this decision?"

"Probably. I'll be honest, Caleb. I love working at my shop. It has been a dream of mine since I was a teen. That's why I took the vocational classes, so I could learn what I needed to do to open and operate the store. Let me ask you a question. At any time during our marriage, when the weather or the market have worked against your plans for your crops, has the money my store allowed me to earn been a consideration for you?"

Caleb paused here. He knew he was entering an area full of painful stickers. "*Ja*. I was always aware of it. Grateful that you had worked hard to earn that money. But I wanted to be the one who earned the money that fed and housed our family. Annie, while I am and have always been grateful for your contributions to our household, there has also been. . . resentment, because I didn't want to have to turn to using your money."

"Caleb! We are in a partnership! What's yours is mine and what's mine is yours. You see other families where the women work, either in the home or out."

Caleb raised one hand. "Wife, I have already consented to this. I'm not going to be able to step over an entire ocean in one giant leap. This is going to take time for me to get used to. Please, don't push me any further."

Annie saw the warning in her husband's eyes. "Okay. We'll wait. But please, take the time to see how it goes with the changes before you make any more decisions. Because we women are able to contribute much to our families and households. I will adjust to coming home in the middle of the day. . . and I suspect I will come to be grateful for that time. As my partner and husband, Caleb, I am asking you to look at your beliefs. Because they are what fueled your attitudes and actions toward Naomi, me and the rest of our daughters. Look at what our married daughters are contributing to their households. Because they are smart, strong women and they are contributing quite a lot."

Caleb nodded. Standing he agreed. "*Ja*. I will think about it. I may never come fully over to your way of thinking, but. . . maybe, in due time, I will be able to accept and understand it."

Sitting back, Annie thought. Then, she nodded slowly. "Okay. I can live with this for now. But. . . what is that English expression? About moving goalposts? Whatever. They will move from time to time. What do you think about meeting with the Yoders?"

Caleb sighed. "Do you want water?" At Annie's nod, he poured both of them glasses of water. Setting hers down in front of Annie, he sat once again. "I guess. I have heard Lizzie Yoder described as some kind of 'fresh breath of air.' And she does look happy much of the time. Jethro seems to treat Naomi well. What will we talk about?"

"Just learning how to see each other as equals and how this affects all areas of our marriage. That's all."

"I guess I can live with that." Sighing, he changed the subject. "So, I guess Naomi is going out again tonight? What ever happened to my little girl that she has become so busy socially?"

"She's friendly and confident. She attracts girls and boys to her. Her relationship with Jethro appears to be much healthier than the others she had before."

"Oh, no, wife. What happened?" Caleb knew he was about to get an earful.

"Her first two boyfriends believed much as you do. One tried to grab her after she broke up with him and jumped out of his buggy. Her first boyfriend didn't try to manhandle her, but he told her that, if they got married, he would make sure she stayed at home. She wouldn't be allowed to work outside the home. That's when she began learning more about what the boys here think about girls, women and how they contribute to their families before she agreed to date Jethro."

"He tried to manhandle her? Who was it?"

"*Nee, Nee*! He and his family moved away. They live in a

settlement in Colorado now." Annie chuckled. "I have to wonder how he and his *daed* feel about that, because from what I hear, that settlement is a little less conservative than what we have here."

"Wife, why didn't she tell me anything?"

"How did you just react?"

Caleb gasped as he understood what Annie was asking. Standing, he looked out the back door, seeing the patterns the bright gold of the sunlight made on the lawn, fence, porch and back swing. He closed his eyes, allowing that image to sink into his soul, calming him down. "Okay, *ja*. I came across as some kind of man who tries to own his wife and daughters."

Annie inclined her head. "I won't disagree. You're already beginning to learn. Naomi learned from her mistakes. She has a good head on her shoulders."

CHAPTER NINE

"Okay. I see exactly what you're saying. So, when we meet with his *mamm* and *daed*, we're just going to discuss, what? More equality?"

Annie nodded quietly, knowing they were entering dangerous ground. "And that's all. They aren't going to try and give us any kind of counseling, because they aren't qualified. I suspect that they are going to simply use their own experiences and what they learned as examples. That's all."

Caleb shrugged. "Let them come by, then. If Jethro and Naomi decide to marry, it seems they're going become a part of our family, anyway. We may as well get to know them."

Annie smiled, feeling deep relief. "*Ja.* Would you like some fruit before supper?"

"That would be *gut*. I am feeling a little like my sugar is low, anyway. If I eat, I may be able to see all these changes in a more positive light." He accepted a pear and an apple from Annie. "*Denki*. I'll be out in the barn." He snagged a napkin on his way out the back door.

Annie sat and thought about what had just transpired. Shaking her head, she knew she was going to have to pull her husband, kicking and screaming all the way, across that path of change.

"*Mamm*, why are you shaking your head? Is everything okay?"

"*Ja*. It is, for now. *Daed* is willing to work with the Yoders. He recognizes the contributions my income has made to the family. He admitted that he resented having to accept my income because he feels that his income should be perfectly sufficient, even in bad farming conditions."

"Well, that's progress of a sort, isn't it? And he admits that he feels kind of. . .*ja*, resentful. What did he say about my new position and your coming home in the middle of the day?"

"He's happy. I suppose I'll get used to it in time. For sure and for certain, I will have more time to get housework done."

"*Mamm*, he needs to know that you've both given something up in gaining what you wanted. You gave up full-time management of the shop. He gave up his dream of making you stay at home full-time. He gets a wife who will be a little more relaxed now. And you get. . . elbow room to keep the store. If he can see that, then you are partway to full agreement with each other."

Annie thought, then slowly nodded. "That's true, isn't it? I'll talk to him about it from that perspective. Maybe the Yoders can start to come and visit before he begins to slip backward again."

Naomi shivered. "I'll talk to them tomorrow, then."

***

The next day's meeting was held at the Yoder's home. After the long service ended, Naomi paired herself with Lizzie Yoder. "Mrs. Yoder, have the elders spoken to you already?"

"*Ja*, indeed they have, my girl! We are going to begin meeting with your parents, right?"

"*Ja*, if you could start sooner rather than later, I would be so grateful. *Daed* got a wake-up call from the elders last week and I don't want him forgetting that."

Lizzie's smile was friendly and open. "No worries, Naomi. I'll speak to Eli this evening. Before Jethro takes you home, we will give you a note with the days or evenings that work best for Eli so your *daed* and *mamm* can decide what night they want to start working with us."

Naomi felt the accumulated tensions of the past several weeks sliding out of her. Her answering smile was shaky. "Denki." After talking with Lizzie Yoder, Naomi sat with Leora and her other friends. Feeling better, she ate the rest of her lunch. Looking around at the summer day, she gave thanks to God for His love and generosity in giving to them.

"Naomi, look. Over there!" Leora had positioned her fork so that it pointed subtly toward Naomi's parents and the Yoders, who had joined the Millers. "It looks like they're going to set up a time to visit your *mamm* and *daed*."

Looking around, Naomi was aware she didn't want others learning of the turmoil that had taken place in her home. She whispered. "*Ja,* I asked them to meet with *mamm* and *daed* earlier rather than later. Let's keep it between us, please."

"I wonder if they would consent to working with my *mamm* and *daed. Daed* is behaving for now, but I just know he'll conveniently forget and start raging on *mamm* and me again."

"After they have agreed on a time with *mamm* and *daed,* why don't you go and ask them for help? Or do you think the elders need to get involved?"

"*Nee.* They're already involved. I think I'll just ask them to start working with them." Leora's eyes moved around, looking for her *daed.* As she observed him, she sighed.

"What's wrong?" Naomi put her fork down.

"Nothing. He actually looks more happy—happier than I have seen him look in a long time! He's visiting with some of the other men, but I don't know what they are talking about. I'll be right back." Leora slid off the bench and hurried toward the house. Coming out, she carried pitchers of water and lemonade. Pouring either beverage into near-empty glasses, she slowly approached her *daed*. "*Daed*, would you like something to drink?"

"*Ja*, daughter! Denki! Lemonade, please."

Leora refilled several other glasses, then returned the pitchers to the house. Returning to her bench, she sat down next to Naomi. "I overheard him talking to one of the other men. They were discussing carpentry stuff. So, as far as I know, he's complying with the elders."

Naomi closed her eyes and whooshed out a deep sigh of relief. "That's *gut*. It sounds like you're keeping a close eye on him."

"*Ja*, I am. *Mamm* can't really, because he'd get too suspicious. But for some strange reason, I can." Leora lapsed into silence as she looked around the crowded benches, seeing what was going on. Families were eating and visiting with one another; children, finished eating, were playing, racing around, throwing a baseball and playing tag. "I'm going to go and talk to Mrs. Yoder. She just went into the kitchen. Right back!" Trotting into the kitchen behind Lizzie Yoder, she ramped up her courage. "Mrs. Yoder?"

"Yes, Leora, how are you?"

"I'm fine, thanks. I was just wondering, would you have time in your schedule to begin meeting with my parents? They are having similar. . . issues... to what the Millers are experiencing."

"*Ja*, the elders spoke to me and I spoke with your *mamm* and *daed*. We will be going to your house after lunch and cleaning up. I am happy to say, your *daed* was agreeable to working with us."

Leora was so relieved that she felt dizzy for a few seconds. Gripping the sturdy kitchen table, she steadied herself. "Oh, thank you! Really, I mean this from the bottom of my heart!"

Lizzie's smile was friendly and understanding. "Let's go into the pantry for a few minutes. I have something to explain to you."

Leora followed Lizzie into the large pantry. "What is it?"

"I have come by my knowledge the hard way. My *daed* used to beat my *mamm* because she wanted to work outside the home to help with the money. He used to tell her that taking care of the house and a large family should have been enough. But she trained us well, so we could help her finish all the work that a large family and home present. And *daed* couldn't always predict when a planting season would go bad. One year. . . well, there were constant rain and windstorms.

One day, we had a horrific tornado and it just ripped through the crops. *Daed* lost almost all of his crops and we were facing financial ruin. He realized that we had no choice but for *mamm* to go to work. She was able to find a job working in a shop like Mrs. Miller's quilt shop. If it hadn't been for her, we would have lost everything."

"Did your *daed* finally stop abusing your *mamm*?"

"*Ja*. He had no choice. The elders visited him and made it very clear that, if he didn't stop hitting her, he would be banned. One of the elders' wives came to our house and she worked with us like I am going to work with your parents and with the Millers."

"Did her work help your parents?" Leora held her breath, waiting for the answer.

"*Ja*. That, in combination with the threat of *Meidung*, forced my *daed* to understand that he could not stand in my mother's way. I realized something long ago, Leora. While we have our ways of doing things here and we stay separate from outsiders, we will struggle with sexism, just like the English do. Do you know what sexism is?"

Leora was stunned. Taking a big gasp, she responded. "*Ja*, I do. Naomi, my friend, her *mamm*, my *mamm* and the other shop employees have been talking about it. We would all agree with you. Our men just don't want to understand that we can be just as successful in providing for our families. We need to be able to bring this topic up in a way that won't violate the *Ordnung*, or we are going to be very busy for a long time."

Lizzie became sober. "I think you are right. Your parents and the Millers are just the tip of the iceberg. And that is what I want to tell the elders—that we need to be on the lookout for other families struggling with this issue and domestic violence."

Leora had heard the term before. "Mrs. Yoder? Is what my *daed* did 'domestic violence?'"

"Leora, call me Lizzie. We are going to be in your home a lot! Yes, he committed a wrongful act of domestic violence against your *mamm*. I know that this is still happening. So, expect to see the elders visiting many more families."

"Lizzie. It isn't just the fathers hitting their wives. I know of at least one instance where some of the teen boys here have either threatened, grabbed or hit their girlfriends. So, they seem to be. . ."

"Picking up on the attitudes of their *daeds*, right?"

"Yes. One of my coworkers is dealing with that now."

"Ach. Is her boyfriend baptized yet?"

"*Nee*. What would the elders do in that situation?"

Lizzie considered. "Well, if they are informed of the violation committed by this boy, they would go and talk to his parents. They might could be able to pick up on whether the boy's *daed* is the root of the problem. If so, we—or another more-enlightened couple—could probably work with them and the boy. What is his name?"

Leora considered the consequences of giving the boy's name out. "I need to talk to my coworker first and let her know.

I think she broke up with him, but I'm not sure."

"*Ja*, please do. If she says yes, then the elders can see what is going on within his family. They might not be able to do very much, since he isn't baptized. But we could begin working with him. Of course, if the elders find that the boy's parents are struggling with domestic violence and an agreement on their roles here, the *daed* could possibly face the ban as well."

"Denki, Lizzie. I will talk to my friend later in the week and I will let you know what she says."

***

On Tuesday, Leora managed to get some private time with Rebecca at the quilt shop. "Rebecca, do you know who the Yoders are?"

"*Ja*. They're Jethro's parents, right? Why?"

"Please keep this between you, me and Naomi. They are working with both of our parents. I hope you won't get mad. But I told Lizzie Yoder what happened to you with your boyfriend."

"I broke up with him. I'm taking your advice and getting to know the boys who are interested in me before I decide to date them or not. It's fine with me if they work with Aaron and his parents. Maybe the next girl he dates won't be subjected to the same treatment I experienced."

"Lizzie told me one thing that really stuck in my head. We

still have some time before we have to go back to work, so I have the time to tell you this: She knows what sexism is. And she told me that, when families are struggling with the roles of husbands and wives, sometimes, the husbands try to keep their wives 'in line' by beating them up. It could be that Aaron learned to treat you poorly from his own *daed*."

Rebecca sighed. Though it was long healed, she began to rub her forearm as though it still hurt. "You know, that night that he grabbed me really scared me. That's what convinced me that I had to break up with Aaron. The few times I was around his *mamm* and *daed*, I did pick up on his *daed* wanting to control what his *mamm* did and what she said. It was very uncomfortable. I asked Aaron to take me home as soon as it was polite enough to do so."

"Do you mind if I take this to Lizzie?"

"Go ahead! I won't be dating Aaron again. And he knows that. I think I disappointed him anyway, because I wouldn't give in and do what he said. He will be single for a long time until he learns that we women have rights, too."

"We need to get back, but I want to talk more with you about this. Okay?"

"*Ja*, that's fine."

Back in the front, the girls returned to work with Naomi in the leadership role. When the store closed at four, Leora and Naomi met up with Vernon, who escorted them to the bank to make the day's deposit.

"I need to get to the market. *Daed* needs some new blades for his saws and I told him I would get them. I'll see you later in the week?"

Leora smiled. "*Ja*, that sounds *gut*! We'll get home okay." After Vernon left them to go to the market, she and Naomi drove to their own homes. "Naomi, I had an idea after talking with Rebecca. She gave me permission to tell you this. Her ex-boyfriend's parents are also dealing with domestic violence because his *daed* won't allow his *mamm* to work outside the home."

Naomi shook her head. "You know, I'm not surprised. I saw Aaron with Rebecca and always thought he was trying to control her. What's your idea?" Naomi already had a suspicion that Leora's idea would be the same as hers.

"We older teen girls need to start communicating to everyone—the boys we're seeing as well as the other boys in Peace Valley—that we are individuals, we are strong and we count. As it is, Lizzie Yoder and her husband already have two couples to work with. At this rate, they'll never stop working with anyone!"

"And if we can start educating the boys and girls our age that violence is wrong, that it violates the *Ordnung* no matter what the intent is, and that we can contribute to our society."

"*Ja*! Exactly! We need to talk to the elders about this. Then to the Yoders, because I want to get started just as soon as possible." Leora finished Naomi's thought.

Both girls were excited, not realizing the resistance they would face.

"Leora, please ask Vernon if we can meet with his *daed* and the other ministers."

***

Later in the week, both girls sat, feeling crestfallen. The bishop had just explained that, while their idea was wunderbaar, several of the families in Peace Valley would not want to change their ways. "Allow us to begin discussing the message that domestic violence is against the *Ordnung*. We will do so over the next few months. Once families realize this, we may get reports of other families like Aaron's. What you two need to do is get like-minded young women and stress the idea that you won't accept being made less than what you are. If you plan to work, either inside or outside the home, hang onto those plans. Get the vocational training you need. And start talking with younger girls, those who are not yet courting or in rumspringa. Because this will not happen overnight."

THE END.

THANK YOU FOR READING!

I hope you enjoyed reading this as much as I loved writing

it! If so, the next book in the Peace Valley series will be available in March 2016. In the meantime, I've put a sample of the Simple Amish Love, another of my books, in the next chapter. You can purchase this book in eBook or Paperback format at your favorite online booksellers.

Also, for a LIMITED TIME, I am offering FIVE of my books for FREE digital download in my Starter Library.

To learn more, go to

FamilyChristianBookstore.net/Rachel-Starter

Or via TEXT MESSAGE send

READRACHELS to 1 (678) 506-7543

to get the Starter Library and updates from me. Make sure to dial the 1 or it won't work. You can also find more of my work at FamilyChristianBookstore.net.

Lastly, if you get a chance to leave me a review, I'd really appreciate it (and if you find something in the book that – YIKES – makes you think it deserves less than 5-stars, drop me a line at Rachel.stoltzfus@globagrafxpress.com, and I'll fix it if I can)

All the best,

Rachel

Be on the lookout for Book Two, coming soon

SIMPLE AMISH LOVE

CHAPTER ONE

"*Mamm*, I've decided I want to be baptized," Annie Fisher announced to her mother one morning after returning from her *rumspringe*, or "running-around" time. In the world of the *Englischers*, she had learned and seen so much – things she loved like dancing and rock music, and things she hated like excess drinking and drugs. She had tried it all – that's what *rumspringe* is for, and she'd found that she wanted the peace and stability of her life at Peace Landing.

"Tell your *daed* so he can let the *Ordnung* know. You do know that you'll need to comply with our community's rules," Annie's mother Mary replied drying her hands on her apron.

"Now that you've returned to Peace Landing, I expect you'll want to decide what you want to do before you begin courting and get married."

"I've also decided about that, too. I want to begin teaching here in the Peace Landing School. I took classes at a community college in New York while I was away."

"*Ach, gut!*" Mary asked, "Have you earned your certificate? It isn't really necessary, but the members of the school board will be more likely to choose you over other candidates if you have it."

"*Ya, mamm*, I know. I hope to be able to go talk to them either next week or the week after," Annie replied. She was glad for those classes in New York; they gave her great teaching tools that would be a positive addition in the community. Different learning styles that children employ, how to remember things better and easier – these and many other techniques made her college jaunt well worth the time.

"Well, tomorrow is a meeting day, so I can let Mr. Kopp know that you are interested in teaching," Mary offered. She looked proud of her daughter, and Annie knew that she was happy that she had returned to the fold. While it was a time to learn about other cultures, most Amish families were happy when their young people chose the traditional life.

"*Mudder*, would you? I . . . I am nervous of approaching him," Annie confessed. It was one of the things that she dreaded most – approaching people even if they were part of her community. She felt awkward, and she would rather get an introduction than going at it cold.

"Annie, he is strict, but a good man. He's fair." Mary folded raisins into the cookie mix she was making. "Please, turn the oven on so I can get these cookies baked before tomorrow. I still need to bake the bread that's rising, so we can take it for tomorrow's lunch." Her mother was encouraging; she wanted her daughter to succeed in her new life. She knew her daughter was naturally shy, but she also knew her daughter had a lot to contribute.

***

The next morning, Annie and her parents rode in their horse-drawn buggy to the Stoltzfus home, where the day's church meeting was being held. Annie was excited, knowing she would be seeing her friends, Jenny Kopp and Ruth Yoder. She shifted restlessly, eager to see them. She looked quickly at the loaves of bread and the box of cookies she and her mother had baked the day before.

Finally, she saw the familiar Stoltzfus property, with the neat, two-story home, the carpentry shop and the fields behind the house. Other buggies had already parked, their horses allowed to graze in the fenced-in field. Annie jumped down before her father could help her down.

Taking the box of cookies from her mother, she walked quickly into the house to set them aside for the community lunch. Walking outside she looked for Ruth and Jenny.

Spotting them waiting for her, a wide smile spread across her gentle, pretty face and she hurried to their sides, *Kapp* strings fluttering in the wind.

"Annie! How was your *rumpspringe*?" Jenny was one of her friends who was, by contrast, outgoing and talkative. She could carry the conversation by herself if she needed to, but she was also considerate of the fact that Annie needed time and space to form and express her thoughts. It was one of the things that Annie liked about their friendship.

"It was . . . interesting, but I was more than ready to return home," Annie said. "I had fun, but I belong here. I'm going to ask for baptism . . . and I plan to ask for a teaching position in the Peace Landing School!"

"I knew it! Ruth, I told you she'd want to teach! Before I came back from New York, she had enrolled in an *Englischer* school to earn her certificate," Jenny was all smiles, her blonde hair creeping out from under her cap as she bounced on her toes.

"Okay, so you were right. Annie, I'll be helping my parents with the *Englischer* tourist business again. We had so much fun with it last summer. And we earned so much money, that will help *Daed* with money for new crops," Ruth smiled and we felt like we were all young again, three girls against the world. We have been friends forever, and now it looks like our friendship will simply pick up where it left off.

"If you need help, let me know. I'll be happy to go to your

farm every day, until school starts," Annie offered.

"Yes! *Mamm* has planned so much! We want to make small quilts for dolls, if you could work on a few," said Ruth.

"Tell your folks I'll help with baking," Jenny offered. "Annie, it was so much fun! And I got to meet Jacob Lapp. We're courting now," Jenny said with a blush and a smile.

"Really? Oh, how exciting! Ruth, how about you? Have you met anybody?" Annie asked.

In response, Ruth blushed and looked down.

Annie grinned. "We'll get it out of you!" she promised. In response she heard a sharp exhale and a "Tuh!"

Looking up, she saw Barbara Kurtz standing in back of Ruth. Her plump stomach strained against the fabric of her dark blue dress. Barbara wore a superior frown. "You girls are so . . . immature. You should be setting your sights on someone more able to provide for a family – someone like Mark Stoltzfus." As she said his name, Barbara's face seemed to melt into a simpering smile, then the smile disappeared and its customary frown reappeared.

Annie shook her head, not wanting to say what she was thinking. "Let's go find seats before service begins. I'd like to sit with both of you," she said instead. The three of them walked quietly to the barn's opening, their happy reunion somewhat marred by Barbara's intrusion. As she walked in between her two closest friends, Annie spotted Mark Stoltzfus, tall and muscular. As he turned and looked at her with a gentle smile, her heartbeat quickened. *Gut, he's still clean-shaven. He's not taken, unless he's seeing someone, but hasn't asked her to marry him.*

"Annie, you're back! I had heard you just returned. How did you like New York?" Mark asked. His blue eyes twinkled and she marveled at the connection they shared. She felt so good, so welcome, back where she belonged.

"It was big, loud, smelly and noisy. I'm glad I got to see the *Englischer* world, but I'm happy to get back home," Annie said truthfully. "I did enjoy it, and I'm glad I got the chance to experience new things – things I would not have gotten to see if I hadn't gone."

"Did you go on tours?"

"*Ya.* I saw the Metropolitan Museum of Modern Art, the 9/11 memorial and other sites. I got used to the subway very quickly! At least, now I know that, when I go back to New York, I will be able to get around," Annie said confidently.

"I enjoyed my time, but I knew I'd be coming back to Pennsylvania and Lancaster county. My life is here, and I'm enjoying starting my own carpentry shop," Mark said.

"It looks like it's time for service to start . . ." Annie said with a shy smile.

"We'll talk later, then," Mark said with an inviting smile.

Annie blushed, hearing the words. Jenny and Ruth took her hands and they found an open bench, where they sat together, listening to that week's minister giving the message. Annie focused on Mr. Yoder as he spoke in his familiar, sing-song Pennsylvania Dutch dialect. At the end of the service, her stomach growled. It had been early when she and her parents had gotten up for breakfast before leaving their house for the day's service. Walking with Ruth and Jenny, she helped bring the foods to the barn, where they were set on long tables set up for the community lunch.

When it was time for the children and young people to sit down and partake of the meal, she was very hungry. Loading her plate with sandwich meats, bread, vegetables, church spread, coffee and *snitz*, she sat down thankfully with her friends and began to eat hungrily. As she looked up from her plate, she saw Mark, at an adjoining picnic table with other young men, looking at her. Looking down, she continued to talk with her friends. Once she had finished eating, she saw Mark walking around, looking for someone. She jumped as Jenny elbowed her in her side. "Mark wants to meet you! He's looking for your parents to ask for permission to court you!"

Annie blushed a delicate rose-pink. She drank deeply from her coffee, not seeing Barbara Kurtz glaring at the three of them.

Barbara glared at them, thinking, *You are not the right person for Mark Stoltzfus! I saw him first, so he's going to be mine. Jenny King, you don't know what "love" is! Ruth Beiler, you're so shy, you'll never court with anyone, let alone get married.* As she thought, one hand stole to her neatly combed hair, sliding under her *kapp* and making sure it was still neatly styled.

Sitting up straight, as she imagined a dignified young woman ready to court might look, she eyed other young women on the picnic benches. None of them had offered to sit with her. None of them was chatting, giggling or gossiping with her. It was just her and her younger sister, Sarah. *So be it. As a young woman of dignity, I am set apart from these giggling . . . schoolchildren.*

"Sarah, I'm going to need your help with something. I want to meet Mark Stoltzfus, and I want him to begin courting me," Barbara whispered.

"How? How will I help you?" Sarah whispered back. Just the thought of mingling with others her age frightened her.

"Never mind. As soon as I get some ideas, I'll let you know what we'll be doing and how you can help me," Barbara whispered back sharply.

Sarah drew away from her older sister – she could be so harsh at times!

***

After dinner that night, Annie had just finished cleaning the kitchen when her father took her arm and asked her to sit at the dinner table.

"We have something to tell you," he said.

"Annie, would you like some tea to go with the oatmeal raisin cookies?" Mary raised her eyebrows expectantly.

"Certainly. I'll boil the water and set the table," Annie said.

Five minutes later, the small family was sitting around the dining room table. Annie nibbled on one of the tasty cookies.

"Annie, you've met Mark Stoltzfus, correct?"

Annie's mouth suddenly went dry. She nodded at her father as she took a sip of her hot, fragrant tea. "*Ya, daed.* We spoke for a few minutes today." She couldn't help but like him; he was beautiful, warm, strong and kind.

"He came to your *mamm* and me after service today, and asked us for permission to begin seeing you. And . . ."

"And, what did you tell him?" Annie asked quietly.

"We told him that he has our permission to begin seeing you. He is a fine young man with a very good head on his shoulders. He will provide a good living to any woman he chooses to marry," John replied.

Annie smiled inwardly, feeling happy. "*Denki, daed!* I . . . I do like him."

"Annie, you are of an age where you can meet young men. Make sure that Mark Stoltzfus is the man you want to start spending time with – seeing multiple men from Peace Landing would not be good for your reputation, especially as you prepare for your baptism," Mary Fisher cautioned.

"*Ya, mamm*, I know. I will not bring shame to the Fisher name," said Annie.

***

After helping her mother with housework the following day, Annie hitched the horse to the buggy and went to visit the Peace Landing school board to request consideration for a teaching position the following autumn.

"My *mamm* is planning to retire at the end of this school year, Mr. Kopp. I have earned my teaching certificate from an *Englischer* college in New York, so I am ready to begin teaching here in Peace Landing," she concluded as she handed her certificate to the school board head.

"Miss Fisher, you have just come back from your *rumspringe*, correct? What decision did you make regarding living in compliance with the *Ordnung*? Do you plan to stay in Peace Landing and make your life here?" asked a junior board member, stroking his short, dark beard.

"*Ya*, Mr. Zook. It is my plan to stay here in Lancaster county and make my life here. The students of Peace Landing will be assured of my presence in the school room every year for as long as God wills it," said Annie quietly.

"Very well, Miss Fisher," said Mr. Kopp. "We will talk amongst ourselves and make our decision before the start of the next school year. Thank you for coming to see us," he said.

Annie stood and shook the hand of each board member. Smiling slightly, she took her leave and left the one-room school house.

***

Annie was finishing the last of her family's ironing when Ruth Beiler and Jenny King stopped by.

"*Mamm*, the ironing is done. May I visit with Jenny and Ruth?" asked Annie.

"Certainly. Ruth, Jenny, you must stay for dinner. We will be having beef stroganoff and vegetables," responded her mother.

"Thank you, Mrs. Fisher. We would appreciate having dinner here," Jenny said with a beaming smile. The three girls walked out to the porch, where they could take advantage of the warm sunlight. Now that spring had arrived, they grabbed every opportunity they could to enjoy the warmth.

"Well . . .?" asked Jenny with a beaming smile.

"Well, what?" asked Annie, teasing her. She knew exactly what Jenny wanted, and she felt like teasing her.

"Come on! What did Mark ask your parents on Sunday?

And what did your parents tell him?"

"Are you going to put a notice in the *Peace Landing Gossip-Gazette*?" asked Annie, with a twinkling grin on her face.

"Annie! What did your *mamm* and *daed* say"

Annie finally decided to stop torturing Jenny. Sighing with a happy grin, she said, "*Daed* and *mamm* gave me permission to start seeing him!"

Annie's friends began squealing in happiness and excitement. Jenny clapped her hands together twice before clasping them under her chin. Happiness showed in her dark brown eyes as her *kapp* slid sideways.

Annie giggled as Jenny set her *kapp* straight. "You're wearing the one that's too big, aren't you?"

"*Ya*. I will tell my *mamm* that it's too big for me to wear. We have fabric, and I can make another one – one that fits!"

After Jenny and Ruth went back home, Annie was helping clean the kitchen when someone knocked on the front door. Her *daed* answered the door, and Annie heard him talking to their guest.

"Well, hello, Mark! Come on in. How was your work today?"

"It was well, *denki*. I have finished a bedroom set for an *Englischer* couple from Philadelphia, and they will pick it up this weekend," said Mark.

In the kitchen, Annie nervously wiped the kitchen counters clean. swallowing a huge lump of nerves that had suddenly settled in her throat. Jumping as she felt her mother's hand land on hers, she looked at her with huge, dark eyes.

"When your *daed* calls you, go into the living room. You have our permission to walk along our property, but stay within sight of the house," Mary murmured.

"*Ya, mamm. Denki*," Annie said. She pushed her *kapp* off her head and smoothed her hands over already-smooth hair, then pulled her *kapp* back on.

"Annie! You have company!" her father called from the living room.

Annie took a calming breath and, smoothing her hands down her dress, she walked into the living room. Seeing Mark, her plastered-on smile smoothed into a more-natural one.

"Hello, Annie. Would you like to take a walk before it gets dark?"

"Yes, *denki*," Annie said.

They walked slowly around the perimeters of the Fisher property. As they walked, they talked about their individual experiences in New York City. Mark was telling Annie about one experience he had on the subways, dealing with an amorous, drunk woman, and Annie, remembering her own subway experiences, laughed in appreciation.

Several yards down the road, Barbara and Sarah Kurtz were in their own father's buggy when Barbara squinted her eyes slightly. As she verified that the man was Mark Stoltzfus, she frowned heavily when she spied the smaller, slender form of Annie Fisher walking next to him. Seeing the couple deep in conversation, she muttered to herself, then told Sarah to hold on tightly. Immediately after, she flicked the horse on a spot she knew was sensitive to the skittish mare – she had flicked this spot several times before, with good effect.

Brownie, the horse, reared and neighed in fright. As her front hooves came down on the packed dirt road, she took off running wildly.

Sarah began screaming in a high-pitched voice, terrified as the buggy bounced and moved down the road. She held onto the side of the buggy, looping her arm through the open window of the buggy. Her other hand gripped Barbara's plump shoulder as she tried to keep her seat.

Mark turned as he heard the high-pitched screams of terror. Seeing the buggy rolling down the road out of control, he told Annie to stay where she was and began running toward the buggy, aiming to meet it so he could grab the reins and stop the runaway horse. Looking to the right, he saw the narrow bridge that bordered the Fisher farm. Reaching desperately, he grabbed the reins and began soothing the horse in a low, calming voice. He dug the heels of his boots into the ground as he forced the horse to stop.

As the buggy came to a sudden halt, Sarah tumbled out because she had been perched so precariously on her seat. As she landed on the hard ground, Mark heard a loud snapping sound as her arm hit the ground. Wincing at the sound, he saw Annie run up and kneel next to the girl. He continued to soothe the still-spooked horse, talking to her in a low voice and running his hand down her sweaty side.

"Miss Kurtz, it looks like your sister has broken her arm. Wait here while Annie goes to my shop to call for medical help." Looking down, he saw Annie rising from the ground.

Annie had heard Mark's brief words to Barbara. Nodding once to Mark, she turned; lifting her skirts slightly and ran to Mark's shop, where she knew a phone was waiting.

"Mark, I'll take her home and we'll get her to a doctor," Barbara said.

"Miss Kurtz, you'll wait. My daughter has already called for help," said John Fisher. "She's already coming back, and my wife is on her way as well."

"But . . ." Barbara whined, feeling embarrassed. She had never intended for Sarah to be hurt. All she had wanted to do was to get Mark's attention and take it away from Annie. "Mr. Fisher, I can take her home and my parents can take Sarah to the clinic . . ."

Annie ran up, breathless. "*Daed*, the clinic in town told us to bring her to them. I called my *Englischer* friend, and she is on her way now. She'll be here in five minutes or less, she said."

Barbara, hearing this, scowled once again. She knew she now owed a debt of obligation to the Fishers, including Annie. Looking from under her heavy eyebrows, she gave Annie a look of dislike.

Mark and Annie, seeing Barbara's reaction, could not figure out why she was so upset that they had taken care of the situation.

THANK YOU FOR READING!

I hope you enjoyed reading this as much as I loved writing it! If so, you can grab this book or the full collection in eBook or Paperback format at your favorite online booksellers.

Also, for a LIMITED TIME, I am offering FIVE of my books for FREE digital download in my Starter Library.

To learn more, go to

FamilyChristianBookstore.net/Rachel-Starter

Or via TEXT MESSAGE send

READRACHELS to 1 (678) 506-7543

to get the Starter Library and updates from me. Make sure

to dial the 1 or it won't work. You can also find more of my work at FamilyChristianBookstore.net.

Lastly, if you get a chance to leave me a review, I'd really appreciate it (and if you find something in the book that – YIKES – makes you think it deserves less than 5-stars, drop me a line at Rachel.stoltzfus@globagrafxpress.com, and I'll fix it if I can)

All the best,

Rachel

ABOUT THE AUTHOR

Rachel was born and raised in Lancaster, Pennsylvania. Being a neighbor of the Mennonite community, she started writing Amish romance fiction as a way of looking at the Amish community. She wanted to present a fair and honest representation of a love that is both romantic and sweet. She hopes her readers enjoy her efforts.

You can keep up with her new releases, discounts and specials and for **LIMITED TIME GET 5 OF HER BOOKS EMAILED TO YOU FOR FREE as a part of Rachel's Starter Library**.

Grab it here:

FamilyChristianBookstore.net/Rachel-Starter

Or get it via TEXT MESSAGE when you send

READRACHELS to 1 (678) 506-7543

BCPL
Baltimore County
Public Library

CPSIA information can be obtained
at www.ICGtesting.com
Printed in the USA
LVOW03s1705080517

533723LV00011B/1328/P

9 781543 151138